In a Free State

V. S. NAIPAUL was born in Trinidad in 1932. He went to England on a scholarship in 1950. After four years at University College, Oxford, he began to write, and since then has followed no other profession. He has published more than twenty books of fiction and non-fiction, including *Half a Life*, *A House for Mr Biswas*, *A Bend in the River* and most recently *The Masque of Africa*, and a collection of correspondence, *Letters Between a Father and Son*. In 2001 he was awarded the Nobel Prize in Literature.

ALSO BY V. S. NAIPAUL

FICTION

The Mystic Masseur
The Suffrage of Elvira
Miguel Street
A House for Mr Biswas
Mr Stone and the Knights Companion
The Mimic Men
A Flag on the Island
Guerrillas
A Bend in the River
The Enigma of Arrival
A Way in the World
Half a Life
Magic Seeds

NON-FICTION

The Middle Passage
An Area of Darkness
The Loss of El Dorado
The Overcrowded Barracoon
India: A Wounded Civilization
The Return of Eva Perón
Among the Believers: An Islamic Journey
Finding the Centre
A Turn in the South
India: A Million Mutinies Now
Beyond Belief
Letters Between a Father and Son
The Writer and the World: Essays
Literary Occasions
A Writer's People: Ways of Looking and Feeling
The Masque of Africa

In a Free State

THE NOVEL

V. S. NAIPAUL

PICADOR

First published 2008 by Picador

This edition published 2011 by Picador
an imprint of Pan Macmillan
20 New Wharf Road, London N1 9RR
Associated companies throughout the world
www.panmacmillan.com

ISBN 978-0-330-52290-8

Originally published 1971 as part of *In a Free State* by André Deutsch.

7 9 8

A CIP catalogue record for this book is available from
the British Library.

Typeset by Intype London Ltd
Printed and bound CPI Group (UK) Ltd, Croydon, CR0 4YY

Visit *www.picador.com* to read more about all our books
and to buy them. You will also find features, author interviews and
news of any author events, and you can sign up for e-newsletters
so that you're always first to hear about our new releases.

A Preface to this Edition

1

In a Free State was conceived in 1969 as a sequence about displacement. There was to be a central novel, set in Africa, with shorter surrounding matter from other places: two fragments from the writer's journal in the Mediterranean and Egypt, and two Indian-immigrant tales (Indian Indian, and Trinidad Indian) from London and Washington. The shorter pieces from these varied places were intended to reinforce and to throw a universal light on the African material.

The programme was clear enough to me, but it turned out to be confusing for other people; and the inclination of Diana Athill, my more than sympathetic reader at the publisher André Deutsch, was to publish the African novel on its own. For a number of reasons I didn't like that idea. I was fresh from the labour of the book. I liked the theme of displacement; I liked the varied backgrounds. Some of the smaller pieces which Diana was willing to throw away hadn't come easily (I had spent three months, working every day, on the revision of one of the immigrant tales). And, above all, I had the idea (which would seem strange to people today) that, since in the main novel I was writing about English expatriates in Africa, and since no one of my background had done so before, it was important for me to define myself. There were not many like me on the literary scene (a handful of Caribbean authors, in the main one-book folk, most already going silent) and I had found, in my thirteen or fourteen years as a published writer, that my background, and my far-away material, had often been contentious issues for publishers, editors, and reviewers. Diana's attitude seemed to be that this was no longer so; but she was prejudiced in my favour.

Diana did not press; the book was published as written. It won the third Booker Prize; and though the Booker in 1971 was not as big as it later became – the original Booker idea was to reward worthwhile books that might be overlooked – the book sold well. And as a result Diana's first idea for a shorter book, without the supporting pieces, fell away. But then, as the years passed and the Booker receded, and the world changed, and I felt myself less of an oddity as a writer, I grew to think as Diana had thought. I felt that the central novel was muffled and diminished by the surrounding material and I began to think that the novel should be published on its own. And this is what, thirty-seven years after its first publication, Picador is doing in this edition, while continuing to publish the fuller version.

2

In a Free State, as sequence, as novel, was conceived and written during a period of intense personal depression that lasted two or three years. It was the last such period in my life; afterwards I was to know serenity. At the time, of course, I had no idea that this serenity was close. And this freezing depression of the writer's – as much as Africa, and perhaps more than Africa – touches everyone in the novel, the bar-boys, the waiters, and even the Africans seen on the road.

The idea of displacement didn't come out of nothing. It reflected my personal situation. In 1964–5 I had bought a small 1840s house in south London. While it was being done up, modestly (large sections of the house were left untouched), I lived in a residential hotel in the Greenwich area. I had no book to keep me creatively occupied. Every terrible day I could reflect on my floating condition. Towards the end of the year, 1965, I got started on a book; and at the same time there came an offer from an American foundation to go to East Africa. I went to Africa; spent nine months there, and finished my book.

When I came back to England I got started on a colonial history of Trinidad. I thought of this as a simple labour. But the subject was engrossing; there was so much about the past of my island I didn't know; the details from the slave time were so awful, so horribly fascinating, it was like looking at another place. It made for a great, taxing labour that took all of two years. During this labour a kind of madness struck me. Having, after great trouble, found a house, I thought that at the end of this new book I should sell my house, leave England, and live a wandering life. I had an idea, light-headed, never examined in any detail, that the new book was going to be successful and would support me.

It didn't, of course, work out like that. Little, Brown, the American publishers who had commissioned the Trinidad book, didn't like what I had written, what I had made of the subject. It took some time for news of their rejection to reach me (this would have been my agent's doing); and so it happened that just a few months after I had left England and started on my wandering life I found myself high and dry. As always in a crisis (in those days), my thoughts turned to writing. I began to write the novel of *In a Free State*.

Three years before, in East Africa, I had often done the spectacular day-long drive from Kampala in Uganda to Nairobi in Kenya. After a day or two in Nairobi at the colonial-style Norfolk Hotel or the newer Panafrica, I would drive back to Kampala. At the end of one of these drives the idea had come unbidden to me (I was working on another book): 'A narrative could be hung on this journey.' This was all the idea with which I had begun the new book. But that idea had begun to bring memories, landscapes, and many pieces of contemporary African history.

My wandering life had at this stage taken me to Victoria, British Columbia. A friend had rented a wonderful clean apartment for me in a brand-new building, and had also rented furniture and china and cutlery. It was a perfect setting for work. Victoria was an old-fashioned civil place. There were Chinese or Korean greengrocers; a good second-hand bookshop. I liked going in for coffee in the morning; and after lunch I went in the other direction to a riding school, hoping to develop this skill to replace my difficult callisthenics before it was too late (this didn't happen). After dinner I walked to the sea. There was a little cove in which, quite mysteriously, as it seemed to me, many long fir logs or poles had been trapped; they tossed with the disturbance of the sea outside, but there seemed no way for them to escape. I could look at the scene for a long time.

And then one day I had nothing to write about. I had come to the end of what I had in my head. Everything about Victoria became then like poison. There was nothing for me to do, but go back to England. I had no house, of course. I stayed in one of the serviced apartments in Dolphin Square. It was expensive, and there was nothing to wait for. After a short while we went to stay with my wife's aunt in the town of Gloucester. She lived in a semi-detached house with a nervous cat that had been abused before it had been rescued by her.

I found the setting restful. On my second day I got out my Victoria manuscript and, braving the cat's unhappiness, sat down in the sitting room to read. I liked what I read. I saw that, six weeks or so before, it was simple nerves that had stopped me going on. I saw now how I could go on. I began to write again. I had intended to stay in Gloucester for only a few days; I found myself staying for many months. At night there were the sounds of a railway marshalling yard, far enough away to be welcome and comforting.

This is the background of the book the reader now holds in his hand. The setting and history is a mixture of Kenya,

Uganda, and Rwanda. Africa changes only slowly. If I were sitting down to write again about the matter of this book I would create the same setting.

In the second half of the novel, after a strange night in a decrepit and now pointless colonial hotel, the main characters prepare to drive home. There is a valley below the main road. The land is muddy and down there, in the mud, with huts smoking with afternoon fires, African women are tilling the land. They are bent at the waist, but straight-legged. It seems an immemorial scene, and the driver of the fleeing car, overwhelmed by the phantasmagoria of the landscape and his own meaninglessness in it, has the idea, which he knows to be strange but which he still cherishes, that at the next bend the modern road he is using will have become an antiquity, overgrown, impassable, while the timeless life of the valley continues below as it did when the road was a living thing.

This little moment was not written in the book I presented to André Deutsch. It had been worked over by me for some days and then abandoned as being too mystical, not in keeping with the rest of the narrative. Many years later I changed my mind. I thought I should use that moment, but I found then that it no longer existed: the manuscript and the original working pages of the book had been destroyed by the warehouse where they had been sent for safe-keeping.

October 2007

In a Free State

1

IN THIS COUNTRY in Africa there was a president and there was also a king. They belonged to different tribes. The enmity of the tribes was old, and with independence their anxieties about one another became acute. The king and the president intrigued with the local representatives of white governments. The white men who were appealed to liked the king personally. But the president was stronger; the new army was wholly his, of his tribe; and the white men decided that the president was to be supported. So that at last, this weekend, the president was able to send his army against the king's people.

The territory of the king's people lay to the south and was still known by its colonial name of the Southern Collectorate. It was there that Bobby worked, as an administrative officer in one of the departments of the central government. But during this week of crisis he had been in the capital, four hundred miles away, attending a seminar on community development; and in the capital there was no sign of war or crisis. The seminar had more English participants than African; the Africans

[3]

were well-dressed and dignified, with little to say; and the seminar ended on Sunday with a buffet lunch in a half-acre garden in what was still an English suburb.

It was like another Sunday in the capital, which, in spite of the white exodus to South Africa and in spite of deportations, remained an English-Indian creation in the African wilderness. It owed nothing to African skill; it required none. Not far from the capital were bush villages, half-day excursions for tourists. But in the capital Africa showed only in the semi-tropical suburban gardens, in the tourist-shop displays of carvings and leather goods and souvenir drums and spears, and in the awkward liveried boys in the new tourist hotels, where the white or Israeli supervisors were never far away. Africa here was décor. Glamour for the white visitor and expatriate; glamour too for the African, the man flushed out from the bush, to whom, in the city, with independence, civilization appeared to have been granted complete. It was still a colonial city, with a colonial glamour. Everyone in it was far from home.

*

In the bar of the New Shropshire, once white, now the capital's interracial pick-up spot, with a reputation for racial 'incidents', the white men wore open shirts and drank beer. The Africans drank shorter, prettier drinks with cocktail sticks and wore English-made Daks suits. Their hair was parted low on the left and piled up on the right, in the style known to city Africans as the English style.

The Africans were young, in their twenties, and plump. They could read and write, and were high civil servants, politicians or the relations of politicians, non-executive directors and managing directors of recently opened branches of big international corporations. They were the new men of the country and they saw themselves as men of power. They hadn't paid for the suits they wore; in some cases they had had the drapers deported. They came to the New Shropshire to be seen and noted by white people, however transient; to be courted; to make trouble. There were no Asiatics in the bar: the liberations it offered were only for black and white.

Bobby was wearing a saffron cotton shirt of a type that had begun to be known as a 'native shirt'. It was like a smock, with short, wide sleeves and a low open neck; the fabric, with its bold 'native' pattern in black and red, was designed and woven in Holland.

The small young African at Bobby's table was not a native. He was, as he had quickly let Bobby know, a Zulu, a refugee from South Africa. He was in light-blue trousers and a plain white shirt, and he was further distinguished from the other Africans in the bar by his cloth cap, of a plaid pattern, with which, as he slumped low in his chair, he continually played, now putting it on and pulling it over his eyes, now using it as a fan, now holding it against his chest and kneading it with his small hands, as though performing an isometric exercise.

Conversation with the Zulu wasn't easy. There too he was fidgety. The king and the president, sabotage in South Africa, seminars, tourists, the natives: he hopped from subject to subject, never committing himself, never relating one thing to another. And the cloth cap was like part of his elusiveness. The cap made the Zulu appear now as a dandy, now as an exploited labourer from the South African mines, now as an American minstrel, and sometimes even as the revolutionary he had told Bobby he was.

They had been together for more than an hour. It was nearly half-past ten; it was getting late for Bobby. Then, after a silence, during which they had both been looking at the rest of the bar, the Zulu said, 'In this town there are even white whores now.'

Bobby, looking at his beer, sipping his beer, not hurrying himself, refusing to meet the Zulu's eyes, was glad that the talk had at last touched sex.

'It isn't nice,' the Zulu said.

'What isn't nice?'

'Look.' The Zulu sat up, his cap on his head, and put his hand to his hip pocket, thrusting forward his small but well-developed chest as he did so, tight within the white shirt. He took out a wallet and flipped his thumb through many new banknotes. 'I could go now to places where this would make me welcome. I don't think it is nice.'

Bobby thought: this boy is a whore. Bobby was nervous of African whores in hotel bars. But he prepared to bargain. He said, 'You are a brave man. Going about with all that cash. I never carry more than sixty or eighty shillings on me.'

'You need two hundred to do anything in this town.'

'A hundred at the outside is enough for me.'

'Enjoy it.'

Bobby looked up and held the Zulu's gaze. The Zulu didn't flinch. It was Bobby who looked away.

Bobby said, 'You South Africans are all arrogant.'

'We are not like your natives here. These people are the most ignorant people in the world. Look at them.'

Bobby looked at the Zulu. So small for a Zulu. 'You must be careful what you say. They might deport you.'

The Zulu fanned himself with his cap and turned away. 'Why do these white people want to be with the natives? A couple of years ago the natives couldn't even come in here. Now look. It isn't nice. I don't think it is nice.'

'It must be different in South Africa,' Bobby said.

'What do you want to hear, mister? Listen, I'll tell you. I did pretty well in South Africa. I bought my whisky. I had my women. You'd be surprised.'

'I can see that many people would find you attractive.'

'I'll tell you.' The Zulu's voice dropped. His tone became conspiratorial as he began to give the names of South African politicians with whose wives and daughters he had slept.

Bobby, looking at the Zulu's tense little face, the eyes that held such hurt, felt compassion and excitement. It was the African thrill: Bobby forgot his nervousness.

'South Africans,' the Zulu said, raising his voice again. 'Over here they never leave you alone. They always look for you. "You from South Africa?" I'm tired of being accosted by them.'

'I don't blame them.'

'I thought you were South African when you came in.'

'Me!'

'They always sit with me. They always want to start a conversation.'

'What a nice cap.'

Bobby leaned to touch the plaid cap, and for a while they held the cap together, Bobby fingering the material, the Zulu allowing the cap to be fingered.

Bobby said, 'Do you like my new shirt?'

'I wouldn't be seen dead in one of those native shirts.'

'It's the colour. We can't wear the lovely colours you can wear.'

The Zulu's eyes hardened. Bobby's fingers edged along the cap until they were next to the Zulu's. Then he looked down at the fingers, pink beside black.

'When I born again –' Bobby stopped. He had begun to talk pidgin; that wouldn't do with the Zulu. He looked up. 'If I come into the world again I want to come with your colour.' His voice was low. On the plaid cap his fingers moved until they were over one of the Zulu's.

The Zulu didn't stir. His face, when he lifted it to Bobby's, was without expression. Bobby's blue eyes went moist and seemed to stare; his thin lips trembled and seemed set in a half-smile. There was silence between the two men. Then, without moving his hand or changing his expression, the Zulu spat in Bobby's face.

For a second or so Bobby's fingers remained on the Zulu's. Then he took his hand away, found his handkerchief, dabbed at his face; and when he put away the handkerchief his eyes were still staring at the Zulu, his lips still seemed set in their half-smile. The Zulu never moved.

The bar had seen. Blacks stared, whites looked away. Conversation faltered, then recovered.

Bobby got up. The Zulu continued to stare, into space now,

never changing the level of his gaze. Deliberately, Bobby moved his chair back. Then, plump and sacrificial-looking in his loose, dancing native shirt, not looking down, left arm at his side, right arm jerking from the elbow, he walked with a fixed smile towards the door.

The Zulu sank lower in his armchair. He put on his cap and took it off; he pressed his chin into his neck, opened his mouth, closed his mouth. His face had been taut and expressionless; now it had the calm of a child. This was what remained of his revolution: these visits to the New Shropshire, this fishing for white men. In the capital the Zulu was a solitary, without employment, living on a small dole from an American foundation. In this part of Africa the Americans – or simply Americans – supported everything.

The liveried barboy, remembering his duties, ran after Bobby with the bill. He stopped Bobby in the doorway, beside the large native drum, part of the new decorations of the New Shropshire. Bobby, at first not hearing, then relieved that it was only the boy, overacted confusion. Feeling below the yellow native shirt for his wallet, in the hip pocket of his soft light-grey flannel trousers, he smiled, as at a private joke, without looking at the boy's face. He gave the boy a twenty-shilling note. Then, absurd chivalry overcoming him, he gave the boy another note, to pay for the Zulu's drinks as well; and he didn't wait for change.

*

In the lobby there was the new official photograph of the president. It had appeared in the city only that weekend. In the old photographs the president wore a headdress of the king's tribe, a gift of the king at the time of independence, a symbol of the unity of the tribes. The new photograph showed the president without the headdress, in jacket, shirt and tie, with his hair done in the English style. The bloated cheeks shone in the studio lights; the hard opaque eyes looked directly at the camera. Africans were said to attribute a magical power to the president's eyes; and the eyes seemed to know their reputation.

From the floodlit forecourt of the New Shropshire – the rock garden, the white flagpole with the limp national flag – Bobby drove down the sloping drive to the dark highway. At night in every suburb the bush began there, on the highway. Every week men of the forest came to settle in the usurped city. They brought only the skills of the forest; they found no room; and at night they prowled the city's unenclosed spaces. There were many frightening stories. Normally Bobby scoffed, rejecting, as much as the stories, the expatriates who told them. But now he drove very fast, down the bush-lined highways, past the wide roundabouts, through the bumpy lanes of the Indian bazaar – houses, shops and warehouses – to the city centre, with its complex one-way system, its half-dozen skyscrapers dark above the bright square and the wide dusty car-park.

In the cramped lobby of his hotel there was again the new photograph of the president, between English fox-hunting prints. The hotel, built in colonial days, was where up-country government officers like Bobby were lodged when they came to the capital on government business. It looked older than it was. Rough timber merged into mock-Tudor: the hotel was partly 'pioneer', partly suburban, still English, home from home. Bobby didn't like it. His room, which had an open fireplace, was white and furry, with white walls, white sheepskin rugs, a white candlewick bedspread and a zebra-skin pouffe.

The evening was over, the week was over. This was his last night in the capital; early in the morning he was driving back to the Collectorate. His packing had already been done. He left a tip for the roomboy in an envelope. Soon he was in bed. He was quite calm.

*

Africa was for Bobby the empty spaces, the safe adventure of long fatiguing drives on open roads, the other Africans, boys built like men. 'You want lift? You big boy, you no go school? No, no, you no frighten. Look, I give you shilling. You hold my hand. Look, my colour, your colour. I give you shilling buy schoolbooks. Buy books, learn read, get big job. When I born again I want your colour. You no frighten. You want five shillings?' Sweet infantilism, almost without language: in language lay mockery and self-disgust.

All week, while being the government officer at the seminar, he had rehearsed that drive back to the Collectorate. But then, at the buffet lunch, he had been asked to give Linda a lift back; and he couldn't refuse. Linda was one of the 'compound wives' from the Collectorate, one of those who lived in the government compound. She had flown up to the capital with her husband, who was taking part in the seminar; but she wasn't flying back with him. Bobby knew Linda and her husband and had even been once to dinner at their house; but after three years they were still no more than acquaintances. It was one of those difficult half-relationships, with uncertainty rather than suspicion on both sides. So the prospect of adventure had vanished; and the drive, which had promised so much, seemed likely to be full of strain.

Disappointment rather than need, then, had sent Bobby to the New Shropshire. And even while he was making his preparations to go out he had known that the evening wouldn't end well. He didn't like places like the New Shropshire. He didn't have the bar-room skills, the bar-room toughness. Instinct had told him, from the first exchange of glances, that the Zulu was only a tease. But he had gone to the table and committed himself. He didn't like African whores. A whore in Africa was a boy who wanted more than five shillings; any boy who wanted more than five was dealing only in money, and was wrong. Bobby had decided that long ago; but he had started to bargain with the Zulu.

That evening he had broken all his rules; the evening had shown how right his rules were. He felt no bitterness, no hurt. He didn't blame the Zulu, he didn't blame Linda. Before Africa, the incident of the evening might have driven him out adventuring for hours more in dangerous places; and then in his room might have driven him to a further act of excess and self-mortification. But now he knew that the mood would pass, the morning would come. Even with Linda as his passenger, the drive remained.

He was awakened by a sound as of crowing cocks. It came from the lane at the side of the hotel. It was one of the sounds of the African night: a prowler had been disturbed, the African hue and cry was being raised. Later, he saw himself again in a place like the New Shropshire. He was on his back and the liveried boy was standing above him; but he couldn't raise his head to see the boy's face, to see whether the face laughed. His head was aching; the pain began to shoot and then it was as if his head were exploding. Even when he awakened, the pain remained, the sense of the drained head. It was some time before he fell asleep again. And when next he was awakened, by the helicopter circling near, then far, then so close it seemed to be directly over the hotel, it was well past five, light in the white room, and time to get up.

2

YAK-YAK-YAK-YAK. The helicopter, flying low, as if examining
the hotel car-park, drowned the braying of the burglar alarm
on Bobby's car as Bobby unlocked the door. Bobby, feeling
himself examined, didn't look up. The helicopter hovered, then
rose again at an angle.

In the bazaar area, through which Bobby had driven so
recklessly the previous evening, the shops and warehouses
of concrete and corrugated iron were closed; the long Indian
names on plain signboards looked as cramped as the buildings.
When the road left the bazaar it ran beside a wide dry gully,
cool now, but promising dust and glare later; and then, the gully
disappearing, the road became a dual-carriageway with flowers
and shrubs on the central reservation.

The Union Club had been founded by some Indians in colonial days as a multi-racial club; it was the only club in the capital
that admitted Africans. After independence the Indian founders
had been deported, the club seized and turned into a hotel for
tourists. The garden was a wild dry tangle around a bare yard.

And in the main doorway, level to the dusty ground, below a cantilevered concrete slab, Linda stood beside her ivory-coloured suitcase and waved.

She was cheerful, with no early-morning strain on her thin face. No need to ask what had kept her overnight in the capital. Her cream shirt hung out of her blue trousers, which were a little loose around her narrow, low hips; her hair was in a pale-brown scarf. In those clothes, and below that concrete slab, she looked small, boyish, half-made. She was hardly good-looking, and she showed her age; but in the Collectorate compound she had a reputation as a man-eater. Bobby had heard appalling stories about Linda. As appalling, he thought, getting out of the car, as the stories she must have heard about him.

With loud words in the empty yard, they fell on one another, conducting this meeting, their first without witnesses, as though they had witnesses; so that all at once, after silence and tension, they were like actors in a play, neither really listening to the other, Linda tinkling, apologetic, grateful, explaining, Bobby simultaneously rejecting explanations and gratitude and fussing tremendously with the ivory-coloured suitcase, as with a stage property.

Yak-yak-yak-yak.

Silenced, they both looked up. The men in the helicopter were white.

'They are looking for the king,' Linda said, when the helicopter moved away. 'They say he's in the capital. He got away from the Collectorate in one of those African taxis. In some sort of disguise.'

Last night's expatriate gossip: Bobby began to be depressed about his passenger. Over rocks and broken pavement they bumped out of the yard.

'I hope they haven't done anything too awful to the poor wives,' Linda said. Her manner was still affected. 'Were you *persona* very *grata* in that quarter?'

'Not very. I'm not a great one for high society.'

She giggled, out of her own cheerfulness.

Bobby set his face. He decided to be sombre, to give nothing away. He had shown goodwill and that was enough for the time being.

Sombrely, then, he drove along the dual-carriageway; and sombrely many minutes later he took the gentle curves of the suburban road, with its wide grass verges, hedges, big houses, big gardens, with here and there now a barefoot yard-boy in khaki.

'You wouldn't believe you were in Africa,' Linda said. 'It's so much like England here.'

'It's a little grander than the England I know.'

She didn't answer. And for some time she said nothing.

He felt he had been too aggressive. He said, 'Of course, they didn't allow Africans to live here.'

'They had their servants, Bobby.'

'Servants, yes.' She caught him unprepared. He hadn't expected her to be so provocative so early. He said, with the calm grim satisfaction of a man prophesying the racial holocaust, 'I suppose that is why someone like John Mubende-Mbarara has refused to move out of the *native* quarter.'

'How well you pronounce those names.'

Bobby's sombreness turned to gloom. 'Well, he won't come to you. If you want to see his work you have to go to him. In the native quarter.'

Linda said, 'When Johnny M. began, he was a good primitive painter and we all loved his paintings of his family's lovely ribby cattle. But he churned out so many of those he got to be a little better than primitive. Now he's only bad. So I don't suppose it matters if he does continue to paint his cattle in the native quarter.'

'That's been said before.'

'About him living in the native quarter?'

'About his painting.' Bobby hated himself for answering.

'He's got awfully fat,' Linda said.

Bobby decided to say no more. He decided again to be sombre and this time not to be drawn.

*

Suburban gardens gave way to African urban allotments with fewer trees, and at the edge of the town the land felt open and the light was like the light that announces the nearness of the ocean. Here, serving both town and wilderness, weathered painted hoardings on tall poles showed laughing Africans smoking cigarettes, drinking soft drinks and using sewing machines.

Allotments turned to smallholdings and secondary bush. A few Africans were about, most on foot, one or two on old bicycles. Their clothes were patched with large oblongs of red, blue, yellow, green; it was a local style. Bobby was on the point of saying something about the African colour-sense. But he held back; it was too close to the subject of the painter.

The land began to slope; the view became more extensive. The Indian-English town felt far away already. To one side of the road the land was hummocked, as with grassed-over ant-hills. Each hump marked the site of a tree that had been felled. Wasteland now, emptiness; but here, until just seventy years before, Africans like those on the road had lived, hidden from the world, in the shelter of their forests.

Yak-yak. At first only a distant drone, the helicopter was quickly overhead; and for a while it stayed, touched now with the morning light, killing the noise of the car and the feel of its engine. The road curved downhill, now in yellow light, now in damp shadow. The helicopter receded, the sound of wind and motor-car tyres returned.

From beside mounds of fruit and vegetables heavy-limbed African boys ran out into the road, holding up cauliflowers and cabbages. There had been accidents here; offending motorists had been manhandled by enraged crowds, gathering swiftly from the roadside bush. Bobby slowed down. He hunched over the wheel and gave a slow, low wave to the first boy. The boy didn't respond, but Bobby continued to smile and wave until he had passed all the boys. Then, remembering Linda, he went sombre again.

She was serene, full of her own cheerfulness. And when she said, 'Did you notice the size of those cauliflowers?' it was as though she didn't know they were quarrelling.

He said, grimly, 'Yes, I noticed the size of the cauliflowers.'

'It's something that surprised me.'

'Oh?'

'It's foolish really, but I never thought they would have fields. I somehow imagined they would all be living in the jungle. When Martin said we were being posted to the Southern Collectorate I imagined the compound would be in a little clearing in the forest. I never thought there would be roads and houses and shops –'

'And radios.'

'It was ridiculous. I knew it was ridiculous, but I sort of saw them leaning on their spears under a tree and standing around one of those big old-fashioned sets. His Master's Voice.'

Bobby said, 'Do you remember that American from the foundation who came out to encourage us to keep statistics or something? I took him out for a drive one day, and as soon as we were out of the town he was terrified. He kept on asking, "Where's the Congo? Is that the Congo?" He was absolutely terrified all the time.'

The road was now cut into a hill and the curves were sharp. A sign said: *Beware of Fallen Rocks*.

'That's one of my favourite road-signs,' Bobby said. 'I always look for it.'

'So precise.'

'Isn't it?'

His sombreness had gone; it would be hard now for him to reassume it. Already he and Linda had become travellers together, sensitive to the sights, finding conversation in everything.

'I love being out this early,' Linda said. 'It reminds me of summer mornings in England. Though in England I never liked the summer, I must say.'

'Oh?'

'I always felt I should be enjoying myself, but I never seemed to. The day would go on and on, and I could never find much to do. The summer always made me feel I was missing a lot. I preferred the autumn. I was much more in control then. To me autumn is the great season of renewal. All very girlish, I'm sure.'

'I wouldn't say girlish. I would say unusual. I once had a psychiatrist who thought we were all reminded of death in October. He said that as soon as he realized this he stopped being rheumatic in the winter. Of course at the same time he'd put in central heating.'

'I somehow thought, Bobby, that you would have a psychiatrist.' She was being bright again. 'Tell me exactly what was wrong.'

He said, calmly, 'I had a breakdown at Oxford.'

He had spoken too calmly. Linda remained bright. 'I've long wanted to ask someone who had one. Exactly what is a breakdown?'

It was something he had defined more than once. But he pretended to fumble for the words. 'A breakdown. It's like watching yourself die. Well, not die. It's like watching yourself become a ghost.'

She matched his tone. 'Did it last long?'

'Eighteen months.'

She was impressed. He could tell.

With a chuckle, as though speaking to a child, he said, 'Look at that lovely tree.' She obeyed. And when the tree had been looked at, he said, solemnly again, 'Africa saved my life.' As though it was a complete statement, explaining everything; as though he was at once punishing and forgiving all who misunderstood him.

She was stilled. She could find nothing to say.

*

This was the famous view. This was the openness the sky had been promising. The land dropped and dropped. The continent here was gigantically flawed. The eye lost itself in the colourless distances of the wide valley, dissolving in every direction in cloud and haze.

Linda said, 'Africa, Africa.'

'Shall we stop and have a look?'

He pulled in where the verge widened. They got out of the car.

'So cool,' Linda said.

'You wouldn't believe you were almost on the Equator.'

They had both seen the view many times and neither of them wanted to say anything that the other might have heard before or anything that was too fanciful.

'It's the clouds that do it,' Linda said at last. 'When we first came out Martin took photographs of clouds all the time.'

'I never knew Martin was a photographer.'

'He wasn't. He'd just got himself a camera. He used to use my name when he sent the film off to be processed, so that no one at Kodak would think he'd taken the pictures. I suppose they must get an awful lot of junk. After he got tired of clouds he began crawling about on his hands and knees snapping toad-stools and the tiniest wildflowers he could find. The camera wasn't built for that. All he got were greeny-brown blurs. The people at Kodak dutifully sent every blur back, addressed to me.'

They were in danger of forgetting the view.

'So cool here,' Bobby said.

A white Volkswagen went past, travelling out of the town. A white man was at the wheel. He blew his horn long and hard when he saw Bobby and Linda, and accelerated down the hill.

'I wonder who he's showing off to,' Bobby said.

Linda found this very funny.

'It's absurd,' Bobby said, when they were sitting in the car again, 'but I feel all this' – he indicated the great valley – 'belongs to me.'

She had been close to laughter. Now she leaned forward and laughed. 'It *is* absurd, Bobby. When you say it like that.'

'But you know what I mean. I couldn't bear looking at this if I didn't know that I was going to look at it again. You know,' he said, sitting up, as stiff as a driving pupil, looking left and right, driving off, 'I never knew a place like Africa existed. I wasn't interested. I suppose, like you, I thought of tribesmen and spears. And of course I knew about South Africa.'

'I've just thought. We haven't heard the helicopter for some time.'

'Helicopters don't have much of a range. It's almost the only thing I learned in the Air Force.'

'Bobby!'

'Just National Service.'

'Do you think they've got the king?'

'It must be awful for him,' Bobby said, 'having to run from the wogs. I am in a minority on this, I know, but I always found him embarrassing. He was far too English for me. We'll see what his smart London friends do for him now. Such a foolish man. I feel sure some of them put him up to all this talk of secession and so on.'

'"I say, awfully stuffy here, with all these wogs, what?"'

'And they found it very charming and funny. I never did, I must say. You know, there's going to be an awful lot of ill-informed criticism. And we won't be exempt. Serving dictatorial African regimes and so on.'

'It's something that worries Martin,' Linda said.

'Oh?'

'The criticism.'

'I am here to serve,' Bobby said. 'I'm not here to tell them how to run their country. There's been too much of that. What sort of government the Africans choose to have is none of my business. It doesn't alter the fact that they need food and schools and hospitals. People who don't want to serve have no business here. That sounds brutal, but that's how I see it.'

She didn't respond.

'It isn't a popular attitude, I know,' he said. 'What is it our Duchess says?'

'Duchess?'

'That's how I call her.'

'You mean Doris Marshall?'

'I bend over "black-wards". Isn't that what she says?'

Linda smiled.

'Very original,' Bobby said. 'But I don't know why we think the Africans don't have eyes. You think the Africans don't know that the Marshalls are on the old South African railroad?'

'She's South African.'

'As she tells everybody,' Bobby said.

'"And proud of it, my dear."'

'"When I was steddying ittykit in Suffafrica –"'

'That's it,' Linda said. 'You've got it exactly. And there's this thing about "glove-box". Do you know about that?'

'You mean you don't say glove-compartment.'

'You always say glove-box.'

'"Because it's ittykit in Suffafrica, my dear."'

'That's it, that's it,' Linda said.

'I think the sooner they finish putting the screws on Denis Marshall and send the two of them packing to South Africa, the better for everybody.'

She rearranged the scarf around her hair and rolled down the window a little.

'It's almost cold,' she said, and took a deep breath. 'That's the nice thing about the capital. The open fires.'

After the way they had just been talking, this expatriate commonplace disappointed him. He said, 'The nicest thing about the capital is this. This drive back. I don't think I'll ever get tired of it.'

'Stop it. You'll make me sad.'

'There's a splendid thing I read by Somerset Maugham somewhere. He's not much admired now, I know. But he said that if you wanted only the best and held out for it, really held out, you usually got it. I must say I've begun to feel like that. I feel we can always do what we really want to do.'

'It's easy for you now, Bobby. But you were saying there was a time when you didn't even know a place like Africa existed.'

'I know now.'

'I know it too. But it doesn't help. I may want to stay, but I know I can't.'

She closed the window and took a deep breath again. She gazed at the wide valley.

She said, 'If I weren't English I think I would like to be a Masai. So tall, those women. So elegant.'

It was a compliment to Africa: he took it as a sign of her new attitude to him. But he said, 'How very Kenya-settler. The romantic blacks are the backward ones.'

'Are they backward? I was thinking of the *manyattas* or whatever they are. Like the drawings in a geography book. You know, your little hut, your tall fence, and bringing home your cattle for the night to protect them against marauders.'

'That's what I meant. Peter Pan in Africa.'

'But doesn't the pre-man side of Africa have this effect on you sometimes?'

He didn't reply. They both became embarrassed.

He said, 'I can't see you in a *manyatta*, I must say.'

She accepted that.

A little later she said, 'Marauders. I love that word.'

The emptiness of the road couldn't now be taken for granted. Traffic to the capital was light but steady: old lorries, tankers driven by turbaned Sikhs, a few European and Asian cars, African-driven Peugeot estate-cars, often looking brand-new, always speeding, packed with rocking Africans.

These Peugeot cars were the country's long-distance taxi-buses. One, horn blaring, surprised and overtook Bobby on a steep slope. The Africans in the back turned round to smile. Linda looked away. The horn continued. Almost immediately the road curved and the Peugeot's brake-lights came on.

'I can't understand why some people like to drive with their brakes,' Bobby said.

Linda said, 'For the same reason that they sell their spare tyres.'

Bend by bend, brake-lights intermittently flashing, the Peugeot pulled away.

'It was one of the things I noticed when I first came out,' Linda said. 'Nearly everybody you met had been in an accident or knew someone who had been in an accident. There were so many people in splints in the compound it looked like a ski resort.'

It was an old joke, but Bobby acknowledged it. 'There was an accident right here not long ago. One of our Singer-Singer Sikh friends turned off his ignition, to coast down. But somehow that locked his steering.'

'What happened?'

'He ran off the road and was killed.'

'Martin says they are the worst drivers.'

'Whenever you see a Mercedes in the middle of the road you can be sure it's an Asian at the wheel. I can't stand those shops. They don't sell the Africans a pack of cigarettes. They sell them just one or two cigarettes at a time. They make a fortune out of the Africans.'

'A good way of getting something out of them is to say, "Hello, isn't this made in South Africa?" They get so terrified they virtually give you the shop free.'

She stopped then, feeling she had gone too far.

*

At last they were at the foot of the cliff and on the floor of the valley. The sun was getting high; the land was scrub and open; it became warm in the car. Linda rolled down her window a crack. At the other side of the valley the escarpment was blurred; colour there was insubstantial, like an illusion of light and distance. They were headed for that escarpment, for the high plateau; and the road before them was straight.

Sixty, seventy, eighty miles an hour: without effort or thought Bobby was accelerating, drawn on by the road. Here, after the hillside windings, the adventure of the drive as speed, distance and tension always began. As he concentrated on the car and the black road, Bobby's sense of time became acute. Without looking at his watch he could measure off quarter-hours.

A derelict wooden building; a warning to slow down, on a washed-out red-and-white roadside board and then in elongated white letters on the road itself. A right-angled turn over the narrow-gauge, desolate-looking railroad track; and the highway became the worn main road of a straggling settlement: tin and old timber, twisted hoardings, a long wire fence with danger signs stencilled in red, dirt branch-roads, trees rising out of dusty yards, crooked shops raised off the earth. And then, making the road narrow, an African crowd.

They wore felt hats with conical crowns and brims pulled down low. Many were in long drooping jackets, brown or dark-grey, which looked like cast-off European clothes. Quite a few, men and women, were brilliantly patched. Two or three men with pencils and pads were marshalling the Africans into open lorries with high canopy-frames. Policemen in black uniforms watched.

'They are restless today,' Linda said.

Bobby, driving very slowly, let the old joke pass. Africans stared from the road and down from the lorries, their black faces featureless below their felt hats. Bobby began a low wave but didn't complete it. Linda, encountering stares, adjusted her scarf and looked straight ahead. Even when they had passed the crowd Bobby continued to drive slowly, anxious not to appear to be running away. In the rear-view mirror the blank-faced Africans with their patches and hats grew small. Out of the settlement, past a curve, Bobby checked again: the road behind showed clear.

The light hurt. Linda put on her dark glasses. The scrub stretched in every direction and seemed to end only with the hazy mountains. In the high sky clouds grew swiftly from the merest white wisps, became silver and black with storm, then disintegrated and reshaped. Bobby and Linda didn't talk. It was some time before Bobby took the car up to speed again.

Linda said, 'You know what they're up to, don't you?'

Bobby didn't reply.

'They are going to swear their oaths of hate. You know what that means, don't you? You know the filthy things they are going to do? The filth they are going to eat? The blood, the excrement, the dirt.'

Bobby leaned over the wheel. 'I don't know how much of those stories one can believe.'

'I believe you know. It's been going on all weekend in the capital.'

'There's an awful lot of gossip in the capital. Some people will insist on their thrills.'

'Hate against the king and the king's people. And against you and me. I can do without that sort of thrill.'

'I know, I know. You think oaths, you think terrorists and *pangas*. But that's not the issue today, thank goodness. And you know, all I believe they do is to eat a piece of meat. I don't think they even eat it. They just bite on it.'

'Well, I suppose going up to Government House to eat dirt and hold hands and dance naked in the dark is no better and no worse than going up to sign the visitors' book.'

She laughed. It broke the mood.

'I must say I didn't like the looks we got there,' Bobby said. 'For a minute it made me feel we were back in the old days. I would've hated to be here then, wouldn't you?'

'Oh, I don't know. I suppose I would have adjusted. I adjust very easily.'

'I wonder whether we aren't a little jealous of the president and his people. At a time like this we feel excluded, and naturally we resent it. I'm sure we would like them a lot more if they were more easygoing. Like the Masai. Speaking personally, I haven't found any . . . "prejudice".'

Above her dark glasses her narrow forehead twitched. 'Oh, it's easy for you, Bobby.'

'What do you mean?'

'I think it's going to rain this afternoon. Just when we leave the tar. I'm looking at those clouds piling up there. If you travel a lot with Martin you get this eye for clouds. That untarred bit of road is my private nightmare. Just half an hour of rain and it's all mud. I can't stand skids. It's like being in an earthquake. It's the one thing that really makes me hysterical. That and earthquakes.'

'I wouldn't say the clouds are "piling up".'

'Still, wouldn't it be romantic if we had to spend the night at the colonel's, watching the rain come sweeping in across the lake?'

'He's very much the sort of character I prefer to keep away from. Everything I hear about him leads me to believe he's a total bore.'

'He's a very settler settler, I must say. He doesn't care for anyone.'

'I suppose you mean Africans.'

'Bobby. Pay attention. The first time the Marshalls went there she asked for a port and lemon.'

'"My dear!"'

'My dear. He just lifted up his scrawny arm and pointed to the door and shouted, "Get out!" Even the barboy jumped.'

'Ittykit in Suffafrica. I forgive him that. I might almost say it's a point in his favour. But why do you say it's easier for me?'

'Oh, Bobby, I've gone over this so often with Martin. We appear to talk of nothing else. When I was a girl lapping up my Somerset Maugham and learning about the great world I never dreamt that so much of my married life would have been spent anguishing about things like "terms of service".'

'Ogguna Wanga-Butere is my superior,' Bobby said. 'He is my – "boss". I show him respect. And I believe he respects me.'

'I'm sorry, but when those names trip off your tongue like that, you make them sound very funny.'

'I very much feel that Europeans have themselves to blame if there's any prejudice against them. Every day the president travels up and down, telling his people that we are needed. But he's no fool. He knows the old colonial hands are out to get every penny they can before they scuttle South. It makes me laugh. We lecture the Africans about corruption. But there's a lot of anguish and talk about prejudice when they rumble our little rackets. And not so little either. We were spending thousands on overseas baggage allowances for baggage that never went anywhere.'

'It was nice to have,' Linda said.

She was abstracted; her good humour had gone. Her bony forehead, curving sharply from the flat, thinning hair below her scarf, had begun to shine; above her dark glasses the worry-lines were beginning to show.

'Busoga-Kesoro brought me the papers. He said, "Bobby, this claim by Denis Marshall has been passed and paid. But we know he didn't take any baggage anywhere this last leave. What do we do?" What could I say? I knew very well there would be talk over the coffee-cups about my "disloyalty". But who are my loyalties to? I told B-K, "I think this should go up to the minister."'

He was exaggerating his role; he was talking too much. He saw that; he saw he was losing Linda's interest. He leaned over the wheel, smiled at the road, shifted about on his seat and said, 'Where shall we stop for coffee?'

'The Hunting Lodge?'

He didn't approve. But he said, 'What a good idea. I hear it's under new management.'

She said in her new abstracted manner, 'After the property scare.'

'The Asians did very well out of that.'

She didn't reply. He fell silent. He would have liked to abolish the impression of talkativeness, to be again, as at the beginning, the man with personality in reserve. But now the sombre person was she.

The road ran black and straight between the flat scrub.

'I believe you are right,' he said after a time. 'The clouds are piling up. At times like this one doesn't know whether to press on or to hang back.'

His manner was conciliating. She made no effort to match it. She said firmly, 'I want coffee.'

They looked at the road.

'I'd heard,' he said, 'that Sammy Kisenyi wasn't the easiest of men. But I didn't know that Martin was so unhappy.'

She sighed. Bobby was stilled; he leaned back against his seat. Then, stilling him further, keeping up the tension, Linda with great weary self-possession rearranged her hair and scarf.

Far away on the road something shimmered. It was more than a mirage. They concentrated on it. A mangled dog.

'I'm glad I've seen it,' Linda said. 'I was waiting for it.' Her tone was mystical. 'You always have to see one.'

'So you'll be leaving?'

'Oh, Bobby, it's so different for you. In your department the work goes on and there's always something to show. But radio is radio. You have to put out programmes. And if you're an old radio man, as Martin is, you know when you are putting out rubbish. And surely the point of coming out here and giving up the BBC was to do something a little better than that. I suppose it's Martin's fault in a way. He was never one of the pushing P.R.O. types.'

'I see that. About the radio. I do feel they overdo the politics and the speeches. There could be a little more editing.'

'When I think that Martin was offered the job of Regional Director. But he said, "No. This is an African country. This is a job for someone like Sammy."'

'They say that Sammy had a rough time in England.'

'Of course it hasn't been a disaster. There are still people in the BBC who remember Martin. When we were there on leave last year someone at the Club said to Martin, "Oh, but you're pretty high-powered over there, aren't you?"'

'But of course. No one spoils his career by coming out here. So you think you'll be going back to England?'

'One has to think of the future. But England: I don't know. Martin has put out feelers here and there. I have no doubt that something will happen.'

'I'm sure it will.' But his question hadn't been answered. He asked, 'Where do you think it'll be?'

He waited.

She said, 'South.'

He said, 'My life is here.'

3

THE SCRUB, when it ruled, had appeared to stretch all the way to the escarpment across a flat valley. But for some time the land had been getting broken and greener. The escarpment still bounded the view, but less and less abruptly. There were now low, spreading, isolated hills; dark trees in the distance hinted at water and streams; here and there hummocked fields spoke of recent forests. Dirt roads began to meet the highway; simple road-signs gave the names of places, twenty, thirty, sixty miles away. There were a few small hoardings. Traffic was still light.

Linda said, in her even mystical voice, 'That's my favourite hill on this drive. It looks as though some giant hand had clawed down the side.'

The description was accurate. It was what Bobby himself felt about the hill.

He said, 'Yes.'

Ahead of them, a tall covered van entered the highway from

a side road. Beagles pushed their heads above the tailboard of the van. Hanging on at the back, badly jolted, were two Africans in jodhpurs and riding boots, red caps and jackets.

'Such a strange part of Africa,' Linda said.

She sat up, took her bag from the floor and brought out her vanity case. She began to make her face up. Her mystical manner had disappeared. Bobby was now the gloomy one.

'When we were in West Africa for those few months,' she said, patting powder, squinting at the hand mirror, 'you would never have said that the Africans there were remotely English. But as soon as you crossed the border into the French place there you saw black men just like ours sitting on the roadside and eating French bread and drinking red wine and wearing little French berets. Now you come here and see these black English grooms.'

The road had begun to curve; the way ahead was no longer clear. They stayed behind the van with the yelping, interested beagles. The grooms eyed the car without friendliness. A sign announced the Hunting Lodge, one mile on.

'We'll have to be quick,' Bobby said. 'I don't like the way those clouds are piling up there.'

'I told you I was the expert.'

The road they turned off into dipped sharply from the embankment of the highway. It ran dark-red and narrow, with deep wheeltracks about a central ridge, between humped fields. Rain had fallen the previous day or early that morning. The car slithered in the wheeltracks; the steering-wheel jumped in Bobby's hands.

'Still hasn't dried out,' Bobby said. 'It must have rained pretty hard.'

'It will rain again soon,' Linda said. But she didn't sound anxious.

The red road curved, following a shallow depression between gentle slopes. Bobby and Linda were enclosed by green; the highway was hidden. Not far ahead of them a line of trees, some white and leafless, marked the course of a stream. Beyond that the land sloped up again, parkland.

'Like England,' Linda said.

'Or Africa.'

Past a turning the land on the left was shaved of humps and was as flat as a swamp, with scattered tussocks of grass and reeds breaking the surface, as in a swamp. At one end of the levelled area was a derelict timber pavilion, the roof partly collapsed.

'Polo,' Linda said.

'Does Martin play?'

As they drove past they saw the ruin in elevation. Light showed through the missing boards in the exposed back wall at the top and between the broken planking of the steps below, so that the pavilion looked like a dark-grey cut-out against the green. The pavilion had not been built to last. It was a structure such as an army might put up and leave behind.

'Do you think those beagles will go back home when the time comes?' Linda said. 'Or will they grow wild?'

The red road ran beside the line of trees, some of which, on the bank of the stream, had died, their roots drowned. Water roared over stones and could be heard above the beat of the car engine. Sometimes the stream itself could be seen, brimming and muddy.

'Goodness,' Bobby said. 'It must have rained heavily.'

The road turned off, twisted and climbed. Broken rocks had been beaten into the road here and they showed jagged where the surrounding earth had been washed away. The car rocked but did not skid; the hill flattened, became open; and they were at the Hunting Lodge: a separate little creosoted office-shed, marked with a board, a mock-pioneer, mock-Tudor hall, and two rows of cottages flat to the ground, with tiled roofs and chimneys and rough casement windows above a profusion of seed-packet flowers drooping from the recent rain.

A white Volkswagen was parked in the yard, the man-oeuvres of its wheels showing fresh on the wet sand. Bobby recognized it as the Volkswagen that had passed them when they had stopped to look at the view. The driver, the man who had sounded the horn, a short, sturdy man of about forty, with dark glasses, khaki slacks and a conventional sports shirt, was waiting.

Bobby, sensing Linda fresh and alert beside him, wondered how he had allowed himself to forget. More, he wondered how he had allowed himself to be brought so directly to the Hunting Lodge. He decided to be grim.

Frowning, he parked.

'Too late for coffee,' the man from the Volkswagen said. He was American, of moderate accent.

'But perhaps in time for lunch,' Linda said.

Bobby, concentrating on his frown and his parking and his general silent grimness, missed his chance to object.

'Bobby,' Linda said, 'do you know Carter?'

Bobby, locking the car door, barely looked up. 'I don't think I do.'

'Well. Bobby, Carter.'

'That's a nice shirt you're wearing, Bobby,' Carter said, taking off his dark glasses, extending a hand.

And Bobby knew he had already been described to Carter by Linda.

'They start serving lunch at twelve,' Carter said. 'But we'll have to order it now if we want it. As you can see, the place isn't exactly packed out. All right, lunch? I'll go and tell her.'

'I'll go,' Bobby said.

He moved off towards the hall.

'In the office, Bobby,' Carter said. 'She's in the office.'

Bobby turned and smiled, as though he knew but had forgotten. Then he thought that it was foolish to smile; and sternly, left arm rigid, soft mouth set, eyes blank, native shirt jumping, he crossed the yard and went up the steps into the little office-shack.

Below the new photograph of the president, with the hair done in the English style, a middle-aged white woman stood writing at a little counter with her left hand. Her right arm was in plaster, in a sling. She looked up as Bobby entered, then went on writing. In another country this would not have been noticeable; here it was unusual. In the corner of the office, out of the light that came through the door, Bobby saw an African. The African was smiling.

The African was dressed like those labourers they had seen that morning being marshalled into the lorries. But his clothes looked more personal and less like cast-offs. His striped brown jacket was stained in many places and the bloated tips of the wide lapels curled; but the jacket fitted. The pullover, rough with little burrs of dirt, fitted; and the shirt, oily and black around the collar, with two or three old tidemarks of sweat, was like a second skin. Seen from the car, the labourers on the road were expressionless and blank, their black faces in shadow below hats pulled down to the crown. But the African in the office carried his round-topped hat in his hand, and his face was exposed. It was a face as plain as the president's in the photograph, showing age alone rather than a quality of experience. Liveliness and emotion lay only in the eyes.

The eyes now smiled, turning from the middle-aged woman writing at the counter to Bobby. When Bobby smiled back the African did not respond. His smile was fixed.

The woman looked up.

'Can we have lunch for three?'

'We start at twelve.'

And then, as though not wishing to show too much interest in Bobby while the smiling African looked on, she returned to her writing.

Bobby didn't see Linda and Carter when he came out of the office. He walked down the gravelled path between the cottages and the drooping flowers. Outside each door there was a little pile of split eucalyptus logs, wet from the rain. An old grey-and-black spaniel was worrying one pile, sniffing loudly. From the cottages the hummocked open land, so recently forest, sloped down to what was still woodland. The stream roared there, its course marked by the bare white branches of those trees whose roots it had drowned.

A forest stream, it turned out, with the forest debris of collapsed trees. But from the high bank on which he stood Bobby saw flat stones and boulders below the raging red water: stepping stones: the small thrills, perhaps, of an ordered garden in a gentler season. A little way up there was a remnant of a retaining brick wall. The stream had long ago breached that and now in flood was making another channel through what had once been a garden, swamping the arum lilies that had grown wild. Sunlight, coming through the trees, lit up some of the white lilies and showed them as patches of pure colour against the tangled weeds pulled flat by the flow of water, silent here, and already in places gathered into stagnant pools.

All at once the lilies lost their brightness; it grew dark below the trees; the swamped garden was silent. The stream raged on. On the other bank tree trunks were black in the gloom; leaves and branches hung low. The wood of a fairy-tale, far from home: what was so recently man-made, after the forests had been cut down and the forest-dwellers flushed out and dismissed, what had perhaps been intended only as an effect of art in a landscape made secure, had become natural. It spoke of an absence of men, danger. Bobby thought of the king, hunted from the sky. He looked up. The rainclouds had massed; the road ahead was untarred for a hundred miles.

He went out of the wood into the open and walked back up the hill. The spaniel was still worrying the pile of split logs and had partly pulled it down. The African with the smile was now outside the office, his hat still in his hand. Bobby acknowledged the African's gaze, turned into the hall and went into the room marked *Lounge*.

It was a long wide room. Small-paned windows with chintz curtains gave clear views of the woodland, the hills beyond with irregular blocks of pine forest, the play of rainclouds. The furniture looked used but not recently used. The new photograph of the president, the man of the forest with his hair now in the English style, stood between coloured prints of English scenes. There were old magazines: photographs of parties, dances, country houses, furniture: an England, as it were, for export, carefully photographed, with what was offending left out. The English countryside Bobby knew best was a spreading semi-industrial confusion of housing developments like tent-cities, old houses lost on busy main roads, railroad tracks, factory buildings; where what remained of Nature – a brook, it might be, with pollarded willows – looked only like semi-urban wasteland. But the room he was in echoed the photographs in the magazines. The scale was too large, for him, for the injured woman in the tiny office; and perhaps it had always been too large.

Someone shrieked: 'Three lunches, was it?'

The shriek, really a hoarse, piercing whisper, came from a middle-aged white man in a state of great ruin. He was bandaged and plastered all the way up one leg and all the way up one arm. He barely supported himself on metal crutches and at every step he seemed about to fall on his face.

'Motor accident,' the man hissed, with some pride. 'They

say lightning never strikes twice . . .' He shook his head. 'You saw my wife?'

'In the office?'

'Got her too.' He leaned forward at a steep angle like a comedian. 'Oh yes. But all right now. Just the itching. Funny thing about plaster. You know, when they take it out at the end, they will still find that little bit at the centre wet. You heading south? Work there? Short-contract man?'

Bobby nodded.

'You're the lucky ones. Sending half back to the London bank every month, eh? Salting it away. But bad in the Collectorate now. Going to be a lot of trouble there, I reckon.'

'I don't know what you mean by trouble,' Bobby said.

The ruined man became guarded. 'No trouble up here.' He nodded to the photograph of the president. 'The witchdoctor's all right. Oh no. No trouble here. Tourism's going to be big business, and the African knows he can't manage it by himself. Say what you like, the African's no fool.'

Bobby put the magazine down and began to move away. He didn't hurry; there was no need. The ruined man started after him, but couldn't pursue.

The African was still outside the office. The spaniel sat, old and blank, on the office steps. The woodpile outside the cottage door had been pulled down. Near it Bobby now saw lavender in bloom, an old bush. As he bent down to break off some spikes he saw, among the scattered logs, a lizard's tail, separate, dead. Then he saw Linda and Carter. Linda waved. It was a large gesture; her blue trousers and cream shirt, seen at a distance, against the gravelled path and the unsettled light of the open hillside, were vivid; and again, as at the start of the day, it was as though they had an audience and were all three in a film or play. Bobby turned: it was only the gaze of the African, cleaning his top lip with his tongue.

Linda said, 'What have you got, Bobby?'

'Lavender.' He passed a spike below her nose. 'I love lavender. Is that effeminate of me?'

She laughed. For the first time he saw her poor teeth. 'I wouldn't say effeminate. I would say old-fashioned.'

She was the brightest of the three when they went into the high timbered dining-hall.

*

They sat at the edge of the desolate room, next to the high fireplace. There was no fire, but logs had been laid. The boy was nervous and abstracted and kept on adjusting the cutlery on the table. His white shirt was less than fresh; his dusty black bowtie was askew.

Carter said, 'You colonialists did pretty well.'

'What a lovely word,' Linda said. 'One so seldom hears it in conversation. You make it sound very big and technical.'

'Sitting here, I feel they must have been very big people. Giants in fact. I suppose that's why they haven't lighted the fire for us. We're too small.'

Or too ugly, Bobby thought, breaking his roll.

The frightened boy brought in the soup plate by plate, pressing his thumbs on the rims. He walked with a stoop, raising his knees high; his big feet, loosely hinged at the ankles, flapped up and down.

'He almost looks like one of ours,' Carter said.

'Carter says there's a four o'clock curfew in the Southern Collectorate, Bobby. The army's rampaging somewhat, apparently.'

'That's what African armies are for,' Carter said. 'They are intended only for civilian use.'

'So it looks as though we'll have to spend the night at the colonel's,' Linda said. 'Or stay here.'

'The "boy" might light the fire for you,' Carter said to Bobby.

Something was wrong with Carter's molars, and he ate like a dog, holding his head over his plate and catching the food in his mouth with every chew, at the same time giving a slight hiss, as though every mouthful was too hot.

He finished a mouthful and made conversation. He said, 'I can't get used to this word *boy*.'

'Doris Marshall tried to call hers a butler,' Linda said.

'Isn't that typical!' Bobby said.

'In the end she settled for steward. It always seems to me such an absurd word,' Linda said.

Bobby said, 'It offended Luke. He said to me afterwards, "I am not a steward, sir. I am a houseboy."'

'Who is Doris Marshall?' Carter asked.

'She's a South African,' Linda said.

Carter looked puzzled.

'Luke is Bobby's houseboy,' Linda said.

'I imagine,' Bobby said, looking at Linda, 'she thought she was bending over black-wards.'

Linda cried, 'Bobby!'

'We are on to my favourite subject,' Carter said. 'Servants.'

Bobby said, 'It always fascinates our visitors.'

Carter ate.

'I can't,' he said later, looking round the dining-hall, once more playing the visitor, 'I can't get over the Britishness of this place.'

'When I was in West Africa,' Linda said, 'everyone was always saying what rotten colonialists we were and how good the French were. And when you crossed the border it looked true. You saw all those black men just like ours sitting on the roadside and eating French bread and drinking red wine and wearing those funny little French berets.'

'So at least,' Bobby said, 'we might be spared over here.'

Carter looked at Bobby and said with direct aggression, 'You do pretty well.'

It began to rain. The dining-hall grew dark; the roof drummed.

'That stretch of mud,' Linda said. 'It's the one thing that makes me hysterical, skidding on mud.'

'I wonder if it's true about the curfew,' Bobby said.

'You don't have to take my word for it,' Carter said.

'I don't have to take your word for anything.'

Linda appeared not to notice. 'Poor little king,' she said, going girlish and affected. 'Poor little African king.'

After this there was nothing like conversation. They finished the bottle of Australian Riesling; and then, to the visible relief of the boy, lunch was over. Bobby seized the bill when the boy brought it. Carter became morose.

'Office,' the boy said. 'You pay office.'

The African was still there, sheltering under the narrow eaves. Rain blurred the edge of the hill, dripped down the tiled roof of the cottages onto the flowers, washed the gravel path. It was almost chilly. Carter was alone in the dining-hall when Bobby went back. They didn't talk; Carter turned and looked out at the rain. Linda, when she came in, was as bright as before.

It was time to leave. Bobby began to fuss.

'I'll stay here for a little,' Carter said.

'Will we be seeing you later perhaps?' Bobby asked.

'Let's leave it open,' Carter said.

Bobby ran through the rain to the car and drove it up to the hall entrance. Linda got in. She looked at Carter; she seemed concerned now. There was some sort of movement in the shadows behind Carter, and the ruined man appeared, leaning forward, as if with exaggerated interest. As Bobby was driving off the woman with the arm-sling came out on the office steps. She gestured towards the African with her uninjured hand and shouted through the rain.

Bobby stopped and rolled down the window.

'Can you take him down to the road?'

'Oh Lord,' Linda said, leaning over the seat to clear her things away.

*

The African opened the door himself. He filled the car with his smell. Through the rain, the windows misting, they drove off, Linda rigid, Bobby wiping the windscreen with the back of his hand. When Bobby looked at the rear-view mirror he caught the African's smiling eyes.

'You work here?' Bobby asked, in the brisk, friendly, simple voice he used with country Africans.

'In a way.'

'What you do? What your work?'

'Anyanist.'

'Oh, you mean *trade* unionist. You *organise* the workers, you *bargain* with the employers. You get your members more money, better conditions. That right?'

'Yes, yes. Anyanist. What you do?'

'I work here.'

'I don't see you.'

'I work in the south. The Southern Collectorate.'

'Yes, yes. South.' The African laughed.

'I'm a civil servant. A bureaucrat. I have my in-tray and my out-tray. I also have my tea-tray.'

'Civil servant. That is good.'

'I like it.'

They were driving slowly down the rocky slope, the rain washing against the windscreen, almost too fast for the wipers. An African came round the corner at the bottom of the slope, walking up to the Hunting Lodge. He saw the car and stood at the side of the road to wait for it to pass. His hat was pulled down low over his head and the lapels of his jacket were turned up.

'He is getting absolutely soaked,' Bobby said, still in his friendly simple voice.

'That is obvious,' Linda said.

'You stop,' the African in the car said to Bobby.

When Bobby looked in the mirror he met the African's gaze.

'You stop,' the African said, looking at the mirror. 'You take him.'

'But he is not going in our direction,' Bobby said.

'You stop. He is my friend.'

Bobby stopped beside the African. Rain ran down the sloping brim of the African's hat; nothing could be seen of his face. Still in the rain, he took off his hat; he looked terrified. The African in the back opened the door. The man came in. He said 'Sir' to Bobby and sat on the edge of the plastic-covered seat until the first African pulled him back.

The Africans made the car feel crowded. Linda rolled down her window and breathed deeply. Rain spattered her scarf.

The level polo ground was awash and now, with the scattered clumps of reeds and grass rising out of the water, looked more than ever like a swamp. Rain had darkened the ruined pavilion.

'Is your friend a unionist too?' Bobby asked.

'Yes, yes,' the first African said quickly. 'Anyanist.'

'I hope you don't have too far to go in this weather,' Bobby said.

'Not far,' the first African said.

Rain splashed the frothing red puddles in the deep wheel-tracks. Sometimes the car slithered. The road began to rise to the high embankment of the highway.

'You turn right,' the African said.

'We are going left,' Bobby said. 'We are going to the Collectorate.'

'You turn right.'

They were now nearly where the red dirt road turned to sand and rock and widened for the last sharp climb to the highway. The African was still looking at the rear-view mirror.

'Is it far, where you want to go?' Bobby said.

'Not far. You turn right.'

'Christ!' Linda said. She leaned back and put her hand to the rear door handle. 'Out!'

Bobby stopped. The wet African, behind Linda, at once jumped out. Almost at the same time the African who had been talking opened his door and got out and put on his hat. Immediately he was faceless, his smile and menace of no importance. Bobby moved up to the embankment, leaving them there, standing on either side of the dirt road, hats pulled down to the shape of their heads, soaking in the rain, two roadside Africans.

'What a smell!' Linda said. 'Absolute gangsters. I'm not going to get myself killed simply because I'm too nice to be rude to Africans.'

Just before he turned into the highway Bobby looked in the mirror: the Africans hadn't moved.

'I've had this too often with Martin,' Linda said. 'It's these damned oaths they're swearing. They feel that everybody's scared stiff of them as a result.'

'But still, it makes me so ashamed. So cocky, and then going just like that. What I can't understand is why he should have hung around for so long up there. You don't have to be from a foundation to find that a little sinister.'

'Sinister my foot. It's just stupidity, that's all. Let's open this window. You can smell the filth they've been eating.'

The rain slanted in, big drops. Bobby, looking in the mirror, saw the Africans standing on the highway. Black, emblematic: in the mirror they grew smaller and smaller, less and less distinct in the rain and against the tar. They began to walk. They walked off the highway, back into the road that led to the Hunting Lodge. Bobby didn't think Linda had seen. He didn't tell her.

4

'IT'S SO PATHETIC,' Linda said.

'I'm sorry. I should have been firmer.'

'You feel sorry for them, and you keep on feeling sorry and saying nice things, nice encouraging things, and before you know where you are you have a Sammy Kisenyi on your hands. I'm afraid we shall have to close the window. The Marshalls talk about the smell of Africa – have you heard her?'

'I should have been firmer.'

'This very special smell.'

'I've never got on with people who talk about things like the smell of Africa,' Bobby said. 'It's like people who talk about, well, the Masai.'

'You may be right. But I used to think I wasn't very sensitive, getting this smell of Africa that the Marshalls and everybody else said they so loved. But I got it this time, when we came back from leave. It lasts about half an hour or so, no more. It is a smell of rotting vegetation and Africans. One is very much like the other.'

It was the smell, in a warm shuttered room, that Bobby liked. He said, 'Perhaps it is time for you to go South.'

'It's so damned pathetic. You remember when the president came to the Collectorate? All those thin and haggard white men, all those fat black men.'

'I don't know why you have this thing about them being fat.'

'I like to think of my savages as lean. You wouldn't believe it now, but Sammy was as thin as a rake when he came back from England. Martin showed the president round the studios. Sammy, of course, doesn't know a microphone from a door-knob. Do you know the first thing Martin said afterwards? It's so embarrassing to say. Martin said, "I'll say this for the witch-doctor. He smells like a polecat." Martin! Well, you know, that sort of thing makes you feel ashamed for everybody, yourself included. But then.'

'Oh dear.'

'Perhaps the word will get around and they'll deport me. I'd like that.'

'Lunch wasn't a good idea.'

'Perhaps not.'

'Your views seem to have changed a good deal since the morning.'

'I don't know whether I have any views really.' Linda's voice was going lighter. 'That's why it would be nice to be deported. We must tell Busoga-Kesoro.'

Bobby didn't like the archness; he didn't like the innuendo. He began to drive fast, too fast for the wet road.

He said, 'They say the animal is always sad afterwards.'

'How romantic, Bobby.'

[53]

He decided to say no more.

The rain thinned. The sky lifted. The road shone in a silver light.

*

An obstruction in the road ahead defined itself as police jeeps, policemen in capes, and two zebra-striped wooden barriers.

Linda said, 'I suppose this is what is known as a roadblock.'

Slowing down, preparing a face for the policemen, Bobby began to smile.

'Please don't be too nice, Bobby. So English those policemen, with their black uniforms and their capes and caps. You can tell that the boss is the fat one, with the plain and fancy clothes.'

It passingly enraged Bobby that the man Linda spoke about seemed to be in charge. He was young and big-bellied; a dark-brown felt hat sat lightly on his head; below a police-issue cape he wore a flowered sports shirt.

With two uniformed policemen he came down the centre of the road to the car.

Bobby said, 'I am a government officer. I'm attached to Mr Ogguna Wanga-Butere's department in the Southern Collectorate.'

The plainclothesman said, 'Licence.'

While he examined Bobby's driving permit his lips and tongue played together, and he held his elbows tight against his sides, giving his paunch a slight lift from time to time.

'My compound pass is on the windscreen,' Bobby said.

'Bonnet and keys, please.'

Bobby pulled the bonnet-release lever and handed over the keys. The uniformed men searched under the bonnet and in the boot, while the plainclothesman himself patted the upholstery on the doors and felt between the seats. He opened Linda's suitcase and pressed down the flimsy contents with a flat, broad hand.

'So' you've been troubled,' he said at last.

It was the formula of dismissal. Then hurriedly, when the car was moving off, like a man remembering part of the drill, he smiled and raised his hat. The hair on which the hat sat so lightly was extravagantly of the English style, scraped together in a high springy mound on one side, with a wide, low parting on the other side.

'It's a consolation anyway that he's one of "ours",' Linda said, as Bobby drove between the zebra-striped barriers. 'But I thought they were looking for the king in the capital, didn't you? The story last night was that he'd got away in one of those taxis.'

'They were looking for arms. I happen to know that there's a lot of concern high up about people smuggling in arms to the Collectorate. Tourists and so forth. They say there's an absolute arsenal in the king's palace. Weren't they extraordinarily polite, though?' The roadblock, the policemen, the rain on the black capes, the open road, his own security: excitement was in Bobby's voice. 'That's Simon Lubero's doing. He's very keen on good relations with the public and so on. Everybody says that Hobbes keeps him up to the mark, but I met him at the conference last year and was most impressed. There was an interview with him in the paper the other day which I found extremely good, I must say.'

'In our own "Two-Minute Silence". Preparing us all. Simon's very British.'

'That's not bad. With him.'

'"So' you been troubled,"' Linda mimicked. 'I feel there must be a curfew, don't you? I know we are white and neutral, but I'm beginning to wonder whether we shouldn't be "racing" in the other direction. We don't seem to have too much company.'

He was in fact racing, half acting out, after the peculiar excitement of the roadblock, a make-believe of danger and escape on the empty African road, lined now on one side with the tall, bare, candelabra-like branches of sisal: the rain almost gone, the clouds high, the light shifting, the rolling land streaked with luminous green, bright colour going on and off on the distant mountains.

He looked at the petrol gauge and said, 'We'll stop at Esher and fill up with petrol.'

'At the time of the Asian boycott everybody in the compound always kept their tanks full, ready to dash off at any moment of day or night to the border.'

'My dear,' Bobby said, 'such excitement. Daily mentions on the BBC, signing on for the airlift at the High Commission, laying in tins.'

'I laid in my tins.'

Linda was showing the effect of the lunch and the Riesling and the drive. Her face was white and strained, dark below the eyes, and the tan on her prominent temples looked like stains, yellow below brown.

She said, abruptly, 'I love this dramatic light, don't you? And the sisal. It all looks so empty until you start seeing those little brown huts. You feel that nothing has ever happened here.' Her voice was going mystical; she was listening to herself speak; Bobby could tell now. 'No one will ever know what has happened here.'

He said, 'Some of us know what happened here.'

'Twenty or thirty people were killed during the Asian boycott. And it wasn't only those Danish dairy experts who were made to double up and down in the sun. I wonder if these things that don't get into the papers or on the radio are reported in some special place, in some little black book. Or big black book.'

Bobby thought: she is not concerned; she is concerned about other things; she is only trying, for no reason, to undermine me, and to transfer her mood to me. Thinking this, he found that his own excitement had gone, that he was waiting to be irritated by her.

'You weren't here for the earthquake,' Linda said. 'I'd just come. The houseboy came to me in the morning with tears in his eyes and said that his family lived in one of the villages that had been destroyed. I took him to the police station, to see whether they had a list of casualties. They didn't, and everybody was very rude. I tried every day for a week. There was no list, and even the houseboy stopped worrying. Nothing in the "Two-Minute Silence". Nothing on the radio. Everybody had just forgotten about it. Was there an earthquake? Did it matter? Perhaps all those people hadn't died, and it didn't matter if they had. Perhaps the houseboy was just trying to make himself interesting. Perhaps nothing that happens here is more interesting than any other thing that happens. Perhaps in a place like this there isn't any news. Sammy Kisenyi can put out the Lord's Prayer every day and call it the news.'

Bobby thought he detected one of Martin's bitter *mots*. But he only said, 'If you put it like that, perhaps there isn't news anywhere.'

'I don't want to argue. I believe you know what I mean.'

'We'll stop at Esher for petrol.'

She said, in half-apology, 'I have a slight head.'

She took her bag from the floor and put it on her knees, looked at her face in her hand mirror and said, 'Good Lord.' Briskly, as though banishing the mood, she made up her face; without weariness, she rearranged her hair and retied her scarf, her arms still young, the short sleeves of her shirt opening to show the mole in her shaved armpit. Then she put on her dark glasses, sat back in her seat and looked quite composed.

Bobby was hating her.

*

ESH, the milestones had been promising every two miles, E S H. And now at last the board – of English design: it might have been imported from England – said ESHER. But there was still only wilderness.

Then old pine trees grew behind wire fences; tractor-marked dirt tracks met the highway in flurries of melting mud. And it was wilderness again. The hills rose in humps on one side; the highway twisted. A washed-out board gave insufficient warning of a level-crossing; the car was jolted. Tall eucalyptus trees made an open, dripping grove, tattered bark on straight trunks; and, against the great mountains in the distance, the rising hills showed a mixture of fenced pastures, hummocked open land, eucalyptus windbreaks, old forest patches: an unfinished landscape, a scratching in the continent.

The verges widened; a few tarnished villas were set in large gardens. There was a roundabout, its garden still maintained, and the highway entered the town. Cross-streets, each with a new black-and-white board bearing the name of a minister in the capital, could be seen to end in mud after two or three hundred yards. The town had been built to grow. It hadn't grown. It remained a collection of old tin-and-timber buildings, its pioneer flimsiness pointed by the small new bank building, the motor car and tractor showroom. The mud-splashed police barracks, low white concrete sheds flat to the ground, already looked like the hutments of the African quarter in the capital.

The filling station Bobby turned into belonged to an oil company that had come to the country after independence. A tall yellow-and-black board announced the amenities in bold international symbols. But one of the symbols, the telephone, had been partly covered over with a square of brown paper; and another symbol, the crossed knife and fork, had been crossed out, apparently by a finger dipped in engine oil. Along the lower edge of the yellow board, as on the white walls of the office, were the marks of oily fingers and sometimes whole hands that had tried to wipe or roll themselves clean. The covered part of the asphalted yard was black with oil; the exposed part, still wet after the rain, was iridescent.

Four Africans in old blue dungarees that looked like cast-offs watched the car come in. When Bobby stopped outside the covered area and sounded his horn, all four Africans started; but then, looking at one another, all four hesitated. One of the Africans was very small; his dungarees dropped low at the crotch and were thick with turn-ups at the ankles.

'I'll go and risk the Ladies',' Linda said.

She walked with fussy little steps, keeping her head down. Her trousers were baggy below the knee and there was a long blot of perspiration on her shirt between the shoulder blades.

The small African and another African came to the car, the small African kicking out at every step, fighting the encumbrance of his dungarees. The small African carried a bucket, a sponge and a metal-handled cleaner. Silently he began to clean the car windows.

Linda came back. 'The place is locked.'

The big African dipped into his pocket and held out a greasy Yale key between a greasy thumb and forefinger. Linda took the key without comment and walked away briskly again.

Oil, petrol, water, battery, tyres: Bobby anxiously super-intended and encouraged the big African. He used his simple friendly voice and he laughed a lot. The African was too pre-occupied to respond. When Linda came back, Bobby went silent. Self-possessed, hard to read behind her dark glasses, she stood at the edge of the asphalted yard, looking across the road to the hills and the mountains.

At last Bobby paid, and he and Linda got back in the car. While they waited for change they were aware of the small African, the cleaner, darkening one window, then another. Linda's forehead began to twitch; she sighed. The big African came with the change. If she sighs again like that, Bobby thought, I'll give her a piece of my mind. The African counted out the change coin by coin into Bobby's hand. It was too much; it was more than Bobby had given.

'It's pathetic,' Linda whispered.

The small African moved from Linda's window to Linda's side of the windscreen. He pulled back the wiper in an alarming way and began to clean, his face level with Linda's and just a few inches away. He frowned, doing his work, making a point of not looking at her.

She looked down at her lap and whispered, 'It's pathetic.'

If she uses that word again, Bobby thought, I'll hit her. He was counting back the excess change into the patient cupped palm of the big African, and he was deliberately counting in his friendly simple voice. He paid out the last coin, which included a tip, and smiled at the African. The big African went away, and the small African came round with his bucket to Bobby's side of the windscreen.

Linda said, 'Look what this one's been doing.'

Bobby looked at Linda's side of the windscreen. Then he looked at the small African. The African was using a double-edged cleaner, one edge made of rubber, one edge made of sponge; but both sponge and rubber had perished, and he was rubbing the central bar of metal on the windscreen. He had left a complicated trail of deep scratches on the windows all around the car. Scratching away now, not looking at Bobby, he frowned, to show his intentness.

Bobby saw the fineness of the African's features, the special, dead blackness of the skin, and recognized him as a man of the king's tribe. Bobby was at once deeply angry. The African, aware of Bobby's scrutiny, frowned harder.

'What on earth do you think you're doing?'

Bobby pushed the door open so violently that the African was hit and thrown off balance.

The African recovered and scrambled away from the car. He said, 'What?' and opened his mouth to say more. But then he just looked at Bobby with shocked, liquid eyes, the disintegrating large sponge in his left hand, the metal-handled cleaner still in his right.

'Look at what you've done,' Bobby shouted. 'You've ruined my windscreen. You've ruined all my windows. You've knocked several hundred shillings off the resale value. Who's going to give me that? You?'

'Insurance,' the African said. And again he seemed about to say something else; but the words didn't come.

'Oh yes, you are very clever. Like all your people. You always know. Insurance? I want it back from you.'

Bobby took a step towards the African. The African stepped back, awkward in his dungarees.

The three other Africans stood still, in their dingy blue dungarees, one next to the door of the office, against the white wall, one in front of the yellow board, one beside the petrol pump.

'I'm going to have you sacked,' Bobby said. 'Sent back to your people. Who's the manager here?'

The African standing against the white office wall raised his hand. He was the man with whom Bobby had dealt, the man who had given the change. He hesitated, then he came towards Bobby. He stood a few feet away, held his hands behind his back and said, 'Manager.'

Company policy, clearly; but Bobby doubted whether this manager had it in his power to recruit and sack.

'I'll be dropping a note to your head office,' Bobby said. He took out an envelope and ballpoint pen from the pocket of his native shirt. 'Who's your superior? Who your boss-man?'

'Dis' sup'indant. Ind-ian.'

'The old Asian trick of remote control. He come here today, your district superintendent?'

'Today no. Home. He live there.' The manager waved towards that part of the town Bobby had just driven through.

'Oh yes, they're all hiding today. Give me his address. Boss-man, where he live?' And while he scribbled on the envelope, with such impatience that he almost immediately stopped writing words and then, deliberately, was just making marks, he said, 'These people shouldn't be employed. They and their king have had it all their own way for too long. But their little games are over now. Look at my windscreen.'

The manager looked, leaning to one side to show that he looked.

The small African had begun to relax within his dungarees.

He was looking down penitentially at the oily yard, still holding his sponge and cleaner, his little mouth set.

Bobby resented this inattention. He said, 'This is something for the police.'

The African looked up, his eyes wide with terror. Again he opened his mouth to talk but said nothing. Then, making a gesture as if he was ready to throw aside the tools of his trade, the sponge and the metal-handled cleaner, he turned and began to walk, kicking out in his dungarees, to the edge of the yard.

'I'm a government officer!' Bobby shouted.

The African halted and turned, 'Sir.'

'How dare you turn your back on me while I'm addressing you?'

Native shirt swinging, crooking his right arm, pulling back his open palm, Bobby advanced on the small African.

The African was making no effort to dodge the blow. There was only expectation in his glittering eyes.

The other three Africans stood where they were, one in front of the yellow board, one next to the pump, the manager near the car.

'Bobby,' Linda said, through the half-open car door. Her voice was neutral, without reproof; she spoke his name as though she had known him a long time.

'How dare you turn your back on me?'

'Bobby.' She had opened the car door and was preparing to get out.

All four Africans stood just where they were as, yellow native shirt dancing, Bobby bustled back to the car. And they remained where they were while Bobby started the car and drove down to the edge of the yard. There he stopped.

'That damned address,' Bobby said. 'Where did I put it?' He acted out an angry search for the envelope on which he had written nothing.

'I think we can forget that,' Linda said.

'Oh no.'

'Drop a note to head office, as you said. I don't think we should go chasing any address that man has given.'

He still searched.

Very quickly, then, with a revving of the engine, a burst of blue smoke and a squeal of tyres, he turned left, heading out of the town, giving up the district superintendent.

The four Africans stood where they were.

*

'The humiliation,' he said, restless in his seat.

Linda said nothing.

The town was quickly past: three or four big concrete sheds and a foundry among the empty overgrown lots of an 'industrial estate', a stretch of bumpy dual-carriageway, washed-out hoardings with their close-to-Caucasian pictures of laughing Africans, the highway again, and then on a hillside rows and rows of unpainted wooden huts, relics of a failed colonial plantation.

'The humiliation.'

Rainclouds darkened the far hills to the right, and the mountains in the distance were hidden. But to the left, where the land was open, the sky was still high, and when the sun struck through the clouds the wet road glistened and the fenced pasture-land was the freshest green.

Suddenly Bobby braked, but with care, without skidding, and pulled in at the side of the road. The road was empty; the manoeuvre was safe. The left wheels sank in soft grass and mud; but he had kept the right wheels on the tar. He bent over the steering-wheel and knocked his forehead lightly against it. Raising his head, resting his right elbow on the wheel, he jammed his palm against his mouth, held his forehead and looked down, and jammed his palm against his mouth again.

'Oh, my God,' he said. 'How awful.'

Clouds raced in the sky. The fields darkened and lit up. Now it was like dusk; now it was afternoon.

'Awful,' he said, hitting his mouth with the heel of his palm. 'Awful.'

He held the wheel with both hands and leaned right over it, the sleeves of the native shirt riding down his arms, pink from the day's exposure.

Linda said nothing. She didn't turn to look. Her dark glasses gave nothing away.

Bobby looked up. 'I know the king's people,' he said. 'He probably is a Christian. He goes to church every Sunday. He keeps his clothes very clean. He washes and irons his own two shirts very carefully. His wife does a little teaching in the school in their village in the Collectorate. He reads. He had that foolish little paperback in the back pocket of those dungarees.' Bobby was thinking of his own houseboy, who was also small and fine-featured and of the king's tribe: a churchgoer and a reader of devout or educational primers in the second, moneyless half of the month, a drinker in the first half, often tortured by hangovers, light and silent then, with an additional quality of delicacy. Bobby said softly, 'God.' Then, leaning again on the steering-wheel, he made himself think of the bar of the New Shropshire. 'God. God.' He looked up. 'God.' But now his voice had changed. 'God, how beautiful.' He was speaking of the play of sunlight in the green field.

At last Linda responded. She turned to look at the field.

Bobby said, 'And now I've destroyed his pathetic little dignity.'

'I don't think so,' Linda said. She saw the tears in Bobby's eyes, and her manner altered. 'I don't think he even knew what it was all about. And anyway they needed a ticking off. It certainly hasn't done them any harm. You should have seen that lavatory. You know, I believe I still have that key.'

'Perhaps I should go back.'

'Whatever for? That would really frighten them. They might even send for the police.'

'I'll probably burst into tears.' His eyes, already clearing up, had just brimmed over. He smiled.

'I doubt it. I think it might get you angry all over again if you went back and found them laughing all over the place.'

'I'll go back.'

'I've been through this so often with my houseboys. You lose a dozen tins of powdered milk, and you tick them off. There is the most terrible scene, and you start walking about your own house on tiptoe. You expect suicide at least, but in the quarters they are having a high old time. They've called in all their friends and they are killing themselves with laughter.'

'We misinterpret their laughter,' Bobby said, his hand playing with the gear lever.

'That may well be. It's embarrassment or disapproval or something like that. Sammy Kisenyi was telling me. And some European probably told him. But I feel that some of it is good old-fashioned laughter.'

Bobby turned on the ignition.

Linda gave a yelp, lifted up her shirt, twisted violently in her seat towards the door.

'I've been stung! See what it is. I can't bear to look.'

Remaining twisted on her left hip, keeping her shirt lifted, she gazed up at the roof through her dark glasses, while Bobby looked. Just below her ribs he saw the red rising bump.

'What is it?' Linda called. 'What is it?'

'I can see where it bit you. But I can't see it.'

'Oh my God.'

She remained rigid and Bobby studied the body which now, like a child, she displayed: the thin yellow folds of the moist skin, the fragile ribs, the brassiere, put on for the day's adventure, enclosing those poor little breasts, and below the waistband of her blue trousers the undergarments that looked as strapped and surgical as the brassiere.

He bent over and kissed the red bump. Linda dropped her eyes from the roof of the car to the top of Bobby's head. She was careful now to hold her shirt up to keep it from covering Bobby's head; and she was also careful to stay still, not to disturb him.

He kissed the bump again and asked, 'Is it better now?'

'It is better.'

He took his head away. She straightened up and dropped her shirt.

'I hope you don't misinterpret my intention,' Bobby said.

'Oh, Bobby, that was one of the nicest things that's ever happened to me.'

'Oh dear,' he said, starting the car. 'You make it sound like childbirth.'

'Women can believe anything.'

She spoke sharply. But it was what he was expecting. It gave the mood a balance; and it was as friends, personalities established, personalities accepted, that they started again on the road.

It became very dark. The black, over-charged clouds were low; the last streak of light on the green field faded. And the rain did come, hard, drowning the sound of the engine, spattering white on the tar. There was no longer a view; there was only rain. It was cosy in the car.

*

'These scratches,' Bobby said. 'I suppose I'll get used to them. I was bitten by my mother's dog once. You can imagine the upset. For me, for my mother, and the poor dog. It was a pretty bad bite. It came out, curiously enough, as two perfectly parallel lines. Just below my calf. The dog is dead now. I still have the marks and, you know, I am rather pleased to have them.'

A little later he said, 'A doctor gave me some tranquillizers once. This was some years ago. I had a recrudescence of my old trouble and I thought I was going to get my breakdown all over again. I don't suppose you ever lose the fear, really.'

'Tranquillizers. Oh dear. Don't tell me you're on those.'

'Listen. He gave me the tranquillizers. Harmless-looking little white tablets. They had a very strange effect. After three days – do you really want me to tell you?' He smiled.

'Do.'

'After three days they burnt the skin off the tip of my penis.'

Linda didn't hesitate. 'How awful for you.'

'Absolutely scorched.' He was still smiling.

*

The rain continued.

'It's strange,' Bobby said. 'I never learned to drive until I came out here. But during my illness I always consoled myself with the fantasy of driving through a cold and rainy night, driving endless miles, until I came to a cottage right at the top of a hill. There would be a fire there, and it would be warm and I would be perfectly safe.'

'Rain outside, fire inside. That's always romantic.'

'No doubt. Very romantic. But it gave me much comfort.' There was a hint of reproof in his voice. 'And then there was this room I saw myself in. Everything absolutely white. White curtains, blowing in with the breeze. White walls, white bed. Lots of tall windows, all open. Outside, the greenest of hills and, at the bottom, a very blue sea.'

'It sounds like a hospital on some Greek island.'

'I suppose it was just that. A wish to give up, to be nothing, to do nothing. Just watching yourself become a ghost. I used to spend hours every day in that room. And every night. I didn't have a bedside table. I used to put my watch on the floor. One morning I stepped on it and broke the glass. I was going to have it mended, but then I changed my mind and decided not to mend it until I got better.'

'Now that is macabre.'

'Walking around with a smashed watch. It's just the sort of sick thing you can do. But the most terrifying thing is how quickly you can adapt to having your whole life written off. At first I used to say, "I'm going to get better next week." Then it was next month. Then it was next year.'

'Isn't there some kind of shock treatment?'

'Like the tranquillizers. I didn't know anything about anything. I thought psychiatry was an American joke and a psychiatrist was someone like Ingrid Bergman in *Spellbound*.'

'It dates us. Wasn't that a gorgeous film?'

'Wasn't it. In a way, you are right about the shock, though. That was how I started to get better. This psychiatrist I used to go to, the one who cured his rheumatism by telling himself he was only frightened of dying, he said to me after one session, "My wife will give you a lift into town." I had never met his wife. I sat in the drawing-room and waited for her. He was that sort of psychiatrist. No surgery, just his house. Perhaps I should have waited somewhere else. I heard this woman talking to some other people. Then I heard her say in her bright voice, "But I can take you in. I've got to take in one of Arthur's young queers." She didn't know I was right there. I thought everything I'd told the man was confidential. I don't believe

I've ever hated anybody so much in my life. I really wanted them both to die. It was unfair really, because he'd done a good job with me. I suppose without knowing it I was getting better. But this shock, as you say, gave me the jolt I needed.'

Linda looked through the scratched glass at the rain.

'"One of Arthur's young queers."' Bobby smiled.

Linda said nothing.

Bobby knew he had embarrassed and moved her. He said, with a touch of aggression, 'I don't believe I've said anything to surprise you?'

'You do terrible things,' he said after a while, the smile gone, his voice altered. 'You do terrible things to prove to yourself that you are a real person. I don't believe I ever felt so exploited.'

'The public attitude has changed a lot.'

'I wonder why. I hate English queers. They are awful and obscene. And then, of course, I was arrested. On a Saturday night, in the usual place. The policeman was niceness itself. He tried to "reform" me. It was funny. He tried to fill my mind with images of desire. It was like an incitement to rape. I thought at one stage he was going to pull out his wallet and show me pornographic pictures. But he did the usual things. He took my handkerchief off me, very carefully. My handkerchief! I could have died with shame. It was a very dirty handkerchief. My case came up early on the Monday morning. After the tarts. Guilty, guilty; ten pounds, ten pounds. I told the magistrate I acted "in the heat of the moment". This caused a little titter and as soon as I'd said it I knew I couldn't have said anything more foolish or damning. But I was discharged very quickly and was able to catch the fast train to Oxford. Oh yes, after my wild London weekend I was back in time for lunch in hall. But I thought Denis Marshall told you. I "broke down" and "confessed" to him some time ago. It always gets me into trouble, but I always break down and confess in the end. It's the effeminate side of my nature. What is it Doris Marshall says they do with people like me in South Africa? They shave our heads, classify us as natives, put us in dresses and send us to live in the native quarter?'

Linda continued to stare at the rain.

'I'm sorry. I've been blabbing as usual, and I believe I've depressed you.'

'I was thinking about the road,' Linda said. 'Even if the mud isn't too bad, I can't see us getting to the compound before eight or nine. I think we should make up our minds pretty quickly whether or not to detour to the colonel's. I was beginning to feel there's something in the settler maxim about aiming to get where you're going by four. It is now half-past two.'

'I haven't heard of anyone starving on the road to the Collectorate.'

'We should make up our mind pretty soon. The turning's going to be on us any minute.'

'No need to ask what your wishes in the matter are.'

'I always think the old colonel's fun,' Linda said. 'And I would love to see the lake in bad weather.'

'I'm glad at any rate that I haven't depressed you. It is nice, isn't it?' he said, speaking now of the landscape. 'Even in the rain, as you say.'

'Driving "through the night" to your little house on the hill.'

'Oh dear. I see that's been taken down in evidence against me. I can't say I'm sorry Denis Marshall's contract isn't going to be renewed. But I don't believe I'll get anyone to believe that it had nothing to do with me.'

'I don't think it matters, Bobby.'

'Busoga-Kesoro brought me the papers. What could I say? We talk so much about corruption among the Africans. And who are my loyalties to, anyway?'

'Doris Marshall can be very amusing. But no one pays too much attention to what she says.'

'It makes me laugh. All the time some people are here they run down the country and criticize the people. As soon as they have to go it's another story.'

'I suppose that's true of me.'

'I didn't mean it like that. I'm sorry that you are going.'

'Why should you be sorry?'

He couldn't say he was sorry because they were in the car together and because he had confessed to her and because she would now always have some idea of him as he truly was.

He said, 'I'm sorry because it hasn't worked out for you.'

'It's different for you, Bobby.'

'You keep saying that.'

'Look. I do believe they've closed the road.'

*

At the road junction, on the road itself, and in the fields about the road, uniformed policemen stood black in the rain with rifles below their capes. Just beyond the junction dark-blue police jeeps blocked the highway to the Collectorate. A red lantern hung from a white wooden barrier; and a black arrow on a long white board pointed down the side road that ran flat to the mountains.

The road to the mountains was clear. No policeman waved Bobby down. But Bobby stopped. Fifty feet or so behind the barrier and the jeeps two heavy planks were laid across the highway: the rain-surf danced about two rows of six-inch metal spikes. A hundred yards or so beyond that, just before the highway curved and was hidden by low bush, there were about half a dozen army lorries with regimental emblems on their tailboards.

Bobby prepared a smile and began to roll down his window. The window-frame dripped, the rain blew in. None of the policemen moved; no one came out of the jeeps. Then a man sitting in the back of a jeep, a fat man, quite young, leaned forward, a chocolate-and-yellow flowered shirt below his cape, and impatiently waved Bobby on; he appeared to be eating.

'Thank God for that,' Linda said. 'I was dreading another search.'

'They're very good that way,' Bobby said. 'They have a pretty shrewd idea who we are.'

'At least they've made up our minds for us,' Linda said. 'Now it will have to be the colonel's. I feel that Simon Lubero's writ ends right here, don't you? The army seems very much in control. I hope we don't run into any of their lorries. They're absolute fiends.'

'I always show the army respect.'

'Martin says that whenever you see an army lorry you must park off the road until it passes. They run you down for fun.'

'I wish they could have kept it a police operation,' Bobby said. 'I'm sure it is what Simon himself would have preferred.'

5

FOR SOME MILES the road to the mountains was asphalted and as wide and safe as the highway they had just left. But this road wasn't built on an embankment; it followed the level of the land which here, near the mountains, had flattened out into the gentlest slope, smooth and bare, without trees. In the openness fenceposts stood out, and the rain-washed road could be seen for some way ahead, empty, skimming the tilted land. The mountains were faint in the rain, but they no longer simply bounded the view; they led the eye upwards.

Fields, fences; a dirt cross-road with a washed-out signpost; a scattered settlement with concrete and timber the colour of wet adobe; trees and bush. The road began to twist and climb. It narrowed. And then there was no more asphalt, only a rough rock surface.

Climbing, they had glimpses of the high plain they had just left; and even through the rain there were suggestions of the land dropping away beyond that. But then, as they went deeper into the mountains, all they saw was the bush on both sides of the road. Curves were sharp around cuttings, wet rock shining below shredded overhangs of roots and earth. There were little, melting landslides in the shallow overgrown ditch and sometimes on the road.

'Really it's hard to know what one would choose,' Bobby said. 'A hundred miles of mud on the highway. Or this.'

Soon they were well into the mountains. Every now and then they saw peaks and further peaks rising above the rain and the mist; so that after only half an hour of climbing it seemed they were on the roof of the world, at the heart of the continent. The sunlight and the scrub, the straight black road, the hiss of the tyres, the play of light on brilliant green fields: that belonged to another country. The car bumped along the rocks; sometimes for stretches the road was strewn with cinders, which made a squelchy sound; the car was noisy, rattling, low gears always above the din of the rain. Not talking, listening for other motor vehicles, half expecting to see army lorries around every blind corner, Bobby and Linda concentrated on the shut-in road.

Occasionally now they saw huts beside the road and wild lilies in small rain-splashed ponds. Sometimes the land fell away on one side and the black trunks of roadside trees and the wet black lower boughs, leaves dripping, framed a view of a grey-green valley: inset terraced hills, red paths going up each hill to a little stockaded grass hut, paths winding away to other, hidden valleys.

'This was what I meant,' Linda said. 'I never expected there would be fields here or that they would terrace up all those hills, right to the very top. I never thought of those tracks, and never thought it would look so old and settled.'

'It was the land we left them,' Bobby said.

She leaned back in her seat and took off her dark glasses, and Bobby saw that he had said the wrong thing, had struck the wrong note.

'It's absurd to think of now,' he said soon after, in another voice. 'I knew nothing at all about Africa when I came here. I was surprised to find them working iron. Somehow no one had thought of telling me that. I was really surprised. But you know that if you leave any old piece of metal lying about –'

'And not so old. Overnight your car can disappear, with only the seats left to mark the spot. They'll pick a Boeing clean in a week.'

Bobby knew the joke, but he laughed. 'I suppose I vaguely felt when I came here that they would be hostile because I was white and English and because of South Africa and things like that.'

'They don't care about South Africa.'

'That's just it. This extreme sophistication. They laugh.'

'Sammy Kisenyi was telling me that's because they're very angry.'

'Sammy exaggerates, like the politicians. Sammy likes to do the racial thing from time to time. He's really just testing you. That can be a bit of a bore. I can't bear that sort of socialistic, third-world pose, can you? It's something he picked up in England. It's not typical. They say Sammy had a rough time in England.'

'It's certainly left him with a thing about the white woman. The blind, the lame, the halt, no one's safe.'

'That's rather pathetic. I wonder how many Sammys we are creating.'

'Pathetic, it's frightening. Sammy believes he's irresistible because he's black and fat. He feels he learned how to "handle" English people in England. Seriously. He's badly mixed up.'

'Sammy's an exception. I suppose what I like about ordinary Africans is that with them there's none of this testing. They take you just as you are. Doris Marshall is right. I have a lot to be grateful to Denis for. He made me come over here. The things you do when you're young. Writing the LCC exam because everybody else was writing it, applying to Hedley's because everybody else was applying. I suppose it's a kind of hysteria. There are so many things you can do perfectly adequately. So many things that you know are not enough, but would do. You look steady, when in fact you're just drifting. I wasn't much of a fighter. After Oxford I was just content to be well again. It never occurred to me that I might want to use myself fully as a human being. It isn't easy to explain, I know, and everything one says can be twisted here. There are too many people around who know how to make the correct noises.'

'You make it so difficult, Bobby.'

'In what way?'

'People take jobs for all sorts of reasons. I wonder if people talk about the place they live in as much as they do about Africa.'

'Oxford. People talked about nothing else except being up at Oxford.'

'I suppose we did try too hard to make the correct noises. We should have known from the first day that the country wasn't for us, and we should have taken our courage in both hands and gone back home.'

'But you've been here six years.'

'As Martin says, the only lies for which we are truly punished are those we tell ourselves.'

'And you're really going South?'

'It's only an idea. In four years Martin will be fifty. I suppose we could go back to England and Martin could go freelance. He is a hack who thinks he is, as Martin says. But you can't really make a fresh start at forty-six. And Martin isn't really the freelance type. He isn't much of a fighter either.'

The car bumped and bumped. The trees dripped. Through black overhanging leaves they had a glimpse beyond far peaks of a small mountain lake, grey, like the sky. A roadside jacaranda had freshly shed its purple flowers, a brushing of delicate colour on the rock and mud of the road: they went over it.

'My life is here.'

'Bobby!'

On a path on the wooded hillside just above the road about a dozen Africans in bright new cotton gowns were walking one behind the other in the rain, covering their heads with leaves. With the bright colours of their cottons, and the leaves over their heads, they were very nearly camouflaged. They didn't look at the car.

'That's the sort of thing that makes me feel far from home,' Linda said. 'I feel that sort of forest life has been going on for ever.'

'You've been reading too much Conrad. I hate that book, don't you?'

'You mean they're probably just going to a wedding or an annual general meeting.'

'Now you sound like Doris Marshall.'

'All right.'

'I loved Denis. I can never stop being grateful to him for what he did for me. My meeting with him at that college Gaudy changed my life. I began to feel I wanted to use myself again. He got me my job here, and I suppose he showed me how to look at the country. But he wanted me to keep on being helpless. He wanted to remain my go-between. He kept on saying that I didn't understand Africans and he would handle them for me. He didn't like it when I started to find my own feet and get around. Such a naïve man, really. He wanted me to remain his property. He went insane when he discovered I didn't object to physical contact with Africans.'

'You were neither of you discreet.'

'He talked so much of service to Africa. I can't tell you how shattered I was. And then he started this campaign against me. I thought I was finished. But that was when I truly got to admire Ogguna Wanga-Butere and Busoga-Kesoro. They understood what Denis was up to.'

'I don't want to hear any more.'

'They are all like that.'

All at once Bobby's excitement died down. He felt he had destroyed the mood of confession and friendship and had lost Linda. He had spoken too much; in the morning he would be full of regret; Linda would be another of those people from whom he would have to hide. He set his face, the silent man.

*

They passed more Africans on the hillside. Linda didn't exclaim or point them out. Bobby began to search for words that would restore the old mood. Half an hour ago he had so many things to say; now nothing new suggested itself. Feeling Linda sitting in reproach beside him, he wished only to go over what he had said, to recapture those passages where he had held her.

'I suppose,' he said, 'this is the sort of drive I used to dream of. The mountains, the rain, the forest. To me it is like Bergman country.'

Yellow mounds of fresh earth began to appear at the roadside and sometimes on the road itself. Heavy vehicles had passed some time before, and their tyres had squashed the earth and spread it over the road; yellow rivulets ran everywhere. Below them there was a valley, grey-green and blurred in the rain. Within the valley there were many conical little hills, each terraced, each with its grass hut behind a grass stockade; and to the huts and along the bottom of the valley faint brown paths ran, like the paths in a fairytale.

'I used to drive day after day along this road and spend hours in that white room –'

'Bobby!'

*

They were skidding, slithering first to the left, the back of the car slapping a mound of earth, the wall of the hillside coming at them, then to the right, the valley clear below them, and it was only the knowledge that the mounds of earth would prevent them going over the precipice that saved Bobby from panic. Then motion became absurd and arbitrary; the car suddenly felt fragile; at every swing it seemed about to overturn. And when at last the car came to rest, they were at a slight tilt in the ditch beside the hillside wall, facing the way they had come, deep in roadside bush, black twigs and wet leaves sticking to the left-hand windows. The engine had cut out; they were aware of the rain on leaves and the car.

Bobby restarted the car and put it in gear. The car bucked and they heard the whine of wheels spinning in mud. He tried again. This time the car didn't buck; they only heard the whine.

Bobby opened his door. Rain and leaves and wind racketed. Stooping, he climbed out onto the road. His yellow native shirt, at first dancing with his brisk movements, quickly became limp and dark with rain.

'There's no damage I can see,' he said to Linda. 'I think it just needs a little push. You take over.'

'I can't drive.'

'Someone will have to push.'

'Can't we wait until some of those Africans we saw turn up?'

'That was miles ago. We'll be well and truly stuck by the time they get here.'

Linda came out through Bobby's door and stood in the gutter behind the spinning wheels. She pushed and then, on Bobby's instructions, she tried to rock the car; and then she simply beat her palms on it. Bobby decided to use the reverse gear. Linda pushed from the front. The reverse gear worked. The car was freed, and Bobby got it back on the road.

Some time later, while Bobby was working the car round to face the way they were going, with Linda moving from one side of the road to another to guide, muddy up to her knees, her shirt wet, her brassiere showing, her hair damp, her hands sticky with mud, some time later the exhaust rammed into a mound of earth and the car stalled. They both then abandoned the car to look for a length of stick to clear the exhaust: the empty car blocking the narrow road at an irrational angle, its occupants soaking and frenzied in separate parts of the bush, Bobby anxious again about army lorries, Linda in the end hysterical, tearing at bush at random and offering Bobby little twigs and sprays, like someone offering herbs.

When they were together again in the righted car they didn't talk. The view was as spectacular as before but they ignored it. The car felt wet and damp; there was mud on the plastic seats and the rubber mats, mud on the floors and dashboard.

'I don't know what idiot dumped this stuff right on the road,' Bobby said.

Linda said nothing.

For miles, it seemed, the mounds of earth continued; and whenever they went over the squashed yellow spread they waited for the car to slip. Without comment they crushed purple jacaranda flowers into the mud. Then there were no more mounds of earth; and then, too, the rain stopped. The sky lightened, became almost silver to the west; and they saw, after the dusk of forest and rain, that it was still only afternoon.

In the valleys there was that stillness that came after prolonged rain. The paths were empty; the depleted clouds, less dark, higher now, didn't move; plants and trees were still. The grey sky was settled: the sun wasn't going to come out again that day. Then, as they drove, they began to see people on the paths, people within the stockades. Smoke rose up straight from some huts.

Always the road followed the contour of a hill; always they had hill and woods on one side. For some time now, in those woods, on paths that had been stamped or beaten into brown-black ledges, they had been seeing Africans on the move, in bright new clothes. The Africans had never been easy to see, with their black skins and multi-coloured cottons. And now Bobby and Linda saw that the hillside along which they had been driving was alive with Africans. Wherever they looked they saw more. On a wide ledge cut into the hill was a low thatched shelter. With its rough leaf-thatch and black poles, trimmed tree-branches, it had at first looked just like part of the woods; but it was packed with seated Africans, all in new clothes. On zigzag paths above and below the shelter many more Africans were standing.

'It's not a wedding,' Linda said. 'It's those oaths of hate again.'

'They're not the president's tribe.'

'They're close enough. Somewhere up there they've taken off their nice new clothes and they're dancing naked and holding hands and eating dung. The president probably sent them a nice piece of dung. You could disappear here without trace. You know what happened on the other side, don't you? The rivers ran red. But that again is something that never happened.'

'They were serfs over there,' Bobby said, his own temper building up. 'They were oppressed for centuries.'

'It's so damned absurd,' Linda said.

He concentrated on the road.

'Not absurd for them. Absurd for me. Being here.'

They had been moving towards the crest of a ridge; the sky felt more open. They came out of the forest on to the bare ridge, and the valley on the other side opened spectacularly: a miniature country laid out below them, every corner filled with the same details of terraced hill and thatched hut, the smoke of cooking-fires, the wet winding paths: a view ending in miniatures of itself, dissolving in mist. The view called for exclamation.

But Linda only said, 'Bergman.'

Bobby set his face.

They began to go down; they lost the view. On this side of the ridge the vegetation was different, more grassy. Some hill-sides were feathery with a fine bamboo. They had a glimpse of the lake they were making for, leaden in the dim light. Then, still going down, they entered woods again and were again in gloom. The road twisted; the ride seemed rougher downhill. There were no signs of men until a cluster of huts and then a villa in a clearing grown wild again announced the nearness of the lake town. By now, in the car, they had exhausted silence and irritation. They had dried out; the mud on the seats and the dashboard was drying fast.

Bobby said, 'Does the colonel give a hot bath?'

'I hope so.' Linda spoke gently.

It was like another turning in the rocky road. But then forest and gloom were abolished and they were out into openness and the light of late afternoon. The lake was before them, wide as the horizon, water indistinguishable from sky. And they were on asphalt again, on a short road that appeared to run right down the hill to the lake, but then turned to show the town and almost immediately became a two-lane boulevard, lamp-standards down the centre, and tall palms, an import, suggesting not the natural growth of the tropics but the nurtured sub-temperate planting of a resort in a colder country.

The boulevard was bumpy. A lamp-standard was broken. A park separated the boulevard from the lake: unlighted cafés on the front, a small, empty pier. On the other side of the boulevard were villas set in enormous gardens, full of colour, startling after the forest. Red bougainvillaea festooned a dead tree. There was an old filling station with one pump; the small window of a tourist shop was choked with ivory and leather objects; on a billboard outside a low, blank building white hand-written posters gave the names of films and actors.

And then, quickly, the town that had looked whole showed

its dereliction. The drives of villas were overgrown, disgorging glaciers of sand and dirt through open gateways. The park was overgrown. The globes and imitation coach-lamps in walls had been smashed and were empty. Metal was everywhere rusty. The boulevard was more than bumpy. It was cracked and fissured; the concrete gutters were choked with sand and dirt and weeds; the sidewalks were overgrown. The roofs of some villas had broken down. One verandah roof, of corrugated iron, was hanging like a bird's spread wing.

The boulevard and park had been cut level in land that was uneven. Almost at the end of the boulevard there was a long mildewed concrete wall, sagging from the pressure of earth on the other side. Above the gateway a vertical board shaped like an arrow with a curving head said HOTEL. They turned in there and went up the concrete incline to the gravelled yard where, next to a strip of old garden that ran parallel with the concrete wall, a large two-storeyed timber building with a built-in verandah still appeared whole.

When they stopped they heard the sound of water. That came from the lake. From the building itself, from a little room near where they had stopped, they heard an English voice shouting.

'That is the colonel,' Linda said. 'He is in form.'

6

THE SHOUTING continued, while Bobby and Linda got their suitcases out of the car and Bobby set the burglar alarm, which immediately cheeped, and then almost brayed as Bobby locked the car door. The shouting continued, but the African who came down the steps from the office, carrying his felt hat in his hand, was smiling; and when he saw Bobby and Linda he smiled more widely. When he put on his hat he became faceless, his smile vanished. His drooping, grimy European-style clothes looked damp; his battered army boots dragged on the wet gravel all the way out of the yard.

Bobby, going up to the office with Linda, set his face. The colonel had heard the car; in the dark office, in a disorder of ledgers and pads, paperbacks and calendars, he was waiting. Set face met set face. The colonel was shorter than Bobby had expected. He was in a short-sleeved shirt and his outstretched hands were pressed against the edge of the counter. The muscles on his arms had shrunk, but he was still powerfully built. He ignored Linda; his dark, moist eyes, full of the strain of his shouting and a rage that had taken him almost to tears, fixed themselves on Bobby.

The colonel wasn't going to speak first. Linda, unrecognized, was also silent.

'We would like two rooms for the night,' Bobby said.

The colonel's gaze dropped from Bobby's face to Bobby's shirt.

A Belgian calendar hung from the pigeonholes on the back wall, above an old black iron safe. There was no photograph of the president, only a framed watercolour of the lake and the hotel, dated 1949 and dedicated by the artist 'to Jim'.

Without speaking, the colonel opened a ledger and turned it to Bobby. Silent himself, his face equally set, Bobby wrote. And it was only while he was writing that he began to understand that the colonel was an old man. The colonel's hands were blotched, the skin loose; they trembled as they pressed against the counter. Bobby was also aware that the colonel was smelling. He saw that the colonel's singlet was brown with dirt; he saw dirt in the oily folds of skin on the colonel's neck.

Bobby passed the ledger to Linda. The colonel stepped back from the counter, turned his head and shouted for the boy. His hands stopped trembling then, and when he turned to Bobby again his face had cleared up; his eyes were even touched with mockery.

He said, 'I take it you'll be wanting dinner?'

'There may be a third person,' Linda said. 'He's probably stuck in those mud heaps on the road.'

This was news to Bobby. And now the set face and the

silence, which he had been addressing to the colonel, served for Linda as well.

They didn't talk as they followed the boy into the main building and up the staircase. The boy was young; the black trousers and red tunic he wore had become, on him, only a type of African clothes; at every step his bare heels popped out of his black shoes. Paint had peeled on the staircase; on the landing there was a stack of old unpainted boards, perhaps discarded shelves; in the dark corridor upstairs, where the jute matting smelled of damp and mould, a bed was stood up on its end. Still without speaking, Linda and Bobby went into their rooms, on opposite sides of the corridor. Linda was the lucky one; she had the room overlooking the boulevard and the lake.

Bobby's room was close and in near-darkness. The rain-spattered window showed the hotel's water-tower, trees and bush, the roofs of buildings in the next street and, in the yard below, the low whitewashed quarters of the hotel boys. Bobby heard the high-pitched chatter in the language of the forest, the banging of pans, the exclamations that were like squeals. No noise came from the rest of the town, over which there hung a faint blue haze, as from scattered cooking-fires.

The bed had been made up some time ago; the bedspread, in a small flowered pattern, had moulded itself to every ridge and hollow of the bedclothes. The top light was dim; on the timber ceiling the hard graining of wood, and knots, showed like burns through the white paint. In the bathroom the fixtures were old and heavy, the washbasin minutely cracked, stained where taps had dripped. The brass fittings in the plug-hole were black. And the water, when Bobby ran it, spat out red-brown with mud: lake water after rain. It didn't get lighter, but it presently ran hot. Bobby washed.

Downstairs someone turned on a radio. An African voice burred and boomed through the hollow wooden building, stumbling over the six o'clock news from the capital, or the comment that followed the news: a voice reading word by word, evenly, and sometimes syllable by syllable, often trapping itself and then impatiently eliding. *'Feu-dal . . . ter'rists . . . se'ssionist . . . Ab'am Lincoln . . . secu'ty forces . . . exte'm'nated . . . vermin.'* The words came up to Bobby like an angry stutter. Against the competition of the radio the hotel boys banged about more and laughed more shrilly and squealed harder and longer in their forest language.

The brown water gurgled away past the black brass outlet into the dark hole, past the flowing strands of slime that were like the ferns at the bottom of a brook; it sent up a rotting smell. The white towel was worn and thin and had a smell of mildew. All at once, drying his face, pressing the towel against his eyes, Bobby felt exhausted, dazed by the long drive; and in that resort town, which he hardly knew, at the edge of that lake, in this hotel room, at this time of day, his exhaustion turned to melancholy.

It was not a disagreeable melancholy. Solitary, he wished now to be alone; he enjoyed the idea of wishing to be alone. It had been a long day; he had talked too much and made many misjudgments. He wished to be absent, to be missed. It was the beginning of one of his sulks; it was so that he punished and refreshed himself.

He didn't change his trousers. He put on the grey shirt he

had worn for the buffet lunch in the capital the day before, and went downstairs. In the bar, where the radio was on, the commentator still angrily entangled in his violent words, there was no light. Above the long concrete wall, on this side no higher than a parapet, the broad spiked palm fronds on the boulevard were black against the lake and the unmoving clouds. In the park, bush hid the wall against which the lake slapped and thumped. Smoke hung faint in the air. The light had almost gone.

Bobby stood in the hotel gateway: he was unwilling to go out on the boulevard. He walked about the yard. He glimpsed cooking-fires in the boys' quarters; women and children looked up; he hadn't expected such numbers. He went and stood in the gateway again. He felt observed. He turned and saw the colonel leaning in a doorway of the unlit bar, looking at him. Bobby went out on the boulevard.

He walked past the hotel's concrete wall; past an empty house, green with damp below a great tree, clods of earth and bits of brick and mortar strewn about the verandah, weeds binding the sand and earth that had flowed out from the drive; and he turned up a side street. The side street was short; the town was only three blocks deep. In the verandah of a villa some Africans were stooped around a cooking-fire. One man, in a tattered army tunic, stood up as Bobby passed. Bobby looked away. But the man had stood up only to throw something from his pocket into the pot.

The town was inhabited. Many of the houses that looked abandoned were occupied, by Africans who had come in from the forest and had used the awkward, angular objects they had found, walls, doors, windows, furniture, to re-create the shelter of the round forest hut. Within drawing-rooms they had built shelters; they had raised roofs on verandah half-walls. Fires burned on pieces of corrugated iron; bricks were the cooking-stones. Many of the men wore ragged army clothes, still wet from the rain, pockets stuffed and drooping. A bicycle leaned in a doorless doorway, as within the stockade of a hut.

On the sidewalks grass had grown around rubbish from the houses, things that couldn't be used and had been thrown out: cracked squares of picture glass, fragments of upholstered chairs, mattresses that had been disembowelled for their springs, books and magazines whose pages had stuck together in solid, crinkled pads. Once Bobby saw a flattened cigarette packet, black on faded red: *Belga*. It recalled European holidays: as though Belgium and Europe had once lain across the water, and the lake had only been a version of the English Channel. This resort hadn't been built for tourists in Africa; it had been created by people who thought they had come to Africa to stay, and looked in a resort for a version of the things of home: a park, a pier, a waterside promenade. Now, after the troubles across the lake, after independence and the property scare, after the army mutiny, after the white exodus South and the Asian deportations, after all these deaths, the resort no longer had a function.

Faintly now, in the distance, there was a rhythmic sound, as of dancing, but so faint that even when Bobby stood still he couldn't be sure. He walked on. At the bush end of a side street he came upon a row of what had once been shops. He heard then the sound of an engine; and a little later a car came banging up the broken street. It was a Chevrolet, driven by an Indian girl. She stopped outside one of the shops. She barely looked at Bobby and hurried in, her high-heeled shoes tapping on the road and the concrete. The shop was in darkness, but it still worked, and was open for business. The shelves were bright with tins; there was a middle-aged man behind the counter.

The rhythmic sound persisted. It became clearer; above it now could be heard a man shouting. Bobby turned back towards the openness of the lake, dead silver through the black of bush and trees and hedges that had begun to grow into trees. But he was walking towards the sound, and the sound itself was coming closer. When he got to the boulevard he saw a company of soldiers coming out at the double into the boulevard from a tunnel of trees. In the dark, and against their shining black skins, the soldiers' white vests glowed like so many white shields; their white canvas shoes were like a separate flutter of pigeon wings. The moustached man shouting at them, and running with them, was in the fatigues of the Israeli army.

Three abreast the soldiers came, khaki trousers, white shoes, white vests, faceless. They had fallen into an easy rhythmic jog. The Israeli, calling time, was running up to the head of the column. There he turned and, continuing to shout, lifting his own legs high, he reviewed the company as they jogged past. But the Israeli was doing one thing, the Africans another. The Israeli was using his body, exercising, demonstrating fitness. The Africans, their eyes half closed, had fallen into a trance-like dance of the forest. Their knees hardly rose; their faces were blank with serious pleasure; they went blinking past the Israeli, blinking away the sweat that rolled down their shaved heads to their eyes. When they had all passed, the Israeli swivelled, still calling 'Ah! Ah!' Then, like a sheepdog, he scampered to the head of the column on the other side, calling to the Africans in vain. The Africans had grown fat and round-armed on the army diet; the Israeli instructor was small, slender, fined down.

Instructor and soldiers continued down one lane of the boulevard; and Bobby, in the other lane, followed them, walking towards the hotel. The jogging white vests came together in the gloom; the white shoes fluttered; then they were hidden by the dark vegetation in the centre of the boulevard. Slowly the tramping receded. But it was always clear, with, above it, the instructor's shout.

And then the tramping and the shouts grew louder again. The soldiers had turned, and were coming down the other lane of the boulevard. A disturbance in the gloom, white growing out of blackness: Bobby stopped to watch. But as the soldiers came near, and shaved heads appeared above bobbing white vests, Bobby became uneasy. It was wrong to stare; he would be noted. So, looking straight ahead, resisting the rhythm of the dance, he walked past the sweating, blinking soldiers and their instructor, who scampered by, inches away, shouting, 'Ah! Ah!'

The night had now fallen. In one or two verandahs African campfires burned low. Some of the street lamps came on, blue, fluorescent. A dim light showed in a villa. On the other side of the boulevard the overgrown park had become the colour of the lake, a flat blackness. Bobby came again to the house with the great tree, its mass suggested by the pale glow of the hotel yard. It was very dark below the concrete wall. Light fanned out through the gateway; the gravelled yard was crisscrossed with shadows. The bar lights were on. Linda was silhouetted in the verandah.

'Bobby?'

He had been missed: she sounded lonely and waiting. She had changed; she was in trousers that were white or cream.

She said in a whisper, 'I feel like a port and lemon.'

But the bar was silent and desolate; and the joke, which had to do with the colonel and Doris Marshall, didn't work.

They sat without talking, sipping sherry, studying the photographs and watercolours on the panelled walls and the dusty Johnny Walker figure on their table. The colonel, now wearing silver-rimmed glasses, sat below one of the ceiling lamps and read a paperback; he was drinking gin. The boy with the red tunic drooped behind the counter, looking down at the counter.

There were footsteps on the gravel, on the concrete steps, on the verandah, and a tall, thin African stood in a doorway of the bar. Below a ragged army raincoat he wore a black suit, a dirty white shirt and a black bowtie; his army-style boots were caked in mud. He stood in the doorway until the colonel looked at him. Then he bowed and said, 'Good evening, Colonel, sir.'

The Colonel nodded and went back to his book.

Tiptoeing in his boots, moving swiftly, not looking at anything in the room, the African went and stood at the bar. The boy poured him a whisky and soda. The African curled thin, long fingers around the glass. As he raised the glass, he rolled his eyes to one side to look at Bobby and Linda.

The colonel went on reading. The silence in the room was like the silence outside.

A motor vehicle hummed in the distance, and then it was in the boulevard. It came closer, its lights lit up the boulevard; it was just outside, it turned into the yard. Two doors banged. Linda, Bobby and the barboy looked at the verandah. It was two Israelis, small, slender men in civilian clothes. They acknowledged the colonel but didn't look at Bobby or Linda. When the barboy went to their table they gave their order without looking up at the boy; and then they spoke softly, almost in whispers, in their own language, like people under orders not to fraternize, comment or see.

One hand in his pocket now, the African finished his drink. Carefully, with thumb and forefinger he placed a coin at the far end of the counter. He stopped near the colonel's table, again waited to be seen, bowed and said, 'Good night, Colonel. Thank you, sir.'

The colonel bowed.

When the African had gone the colonel looked at Bobby and Linda over his glasses and said with what might have been a smile, 'Well, at least some of us still dress.'

Linda smiled.

Bobby set his face, and he had the satisfaction of seeing the colonel give up his attempt at a smile.

'You don't have to tell me what your rooms are like,' the colonel said. 'I haven't been up those stairs for three or four months.' He put one hand to his hip. 'Peter looks after that now. Head boy. You should see his quarters. Used to inspect the quarters once a month. Gave that up years ago. Couldn't bear it. What's the use, what's the use?' Holding the paperback in both hands, flexing the spine, he began to read again.

A tall liveried boy came in from the adjoining room and said to the colonel, 'Dinner, sir.'

The two Israelis got up at once and went in with their drinks.

Linda said, 'I'll go upstairs for a moment.'

Bobby didn't wait in the bar. He went into the dining-room. It was a large open room with two square pillars in the middle and wide wire-netted windows in the wall that faced the lake. The panelled side walls were hung with more watercolours. There were about twelve tables and all were laid. Half a dozen sauce bottles, a tall silver cruet-stand and a stack of books and magazines marked the colonel's table. The table to which the boy led Bobby was laid for three.

The boy was big and he moved briskly, creating little turbulences of stink. The cuffs and collar of his red tunic were oily black; oil gleamed on his cheeks and neck. The menu he gave Bobby was written out in a strong old-fashioned sloping hand: five courses.

Linda came back.

'That was quick,' Bobby said.

She took the menu and frowned hard at it. 'I saw someone in your room.'

She continued to frown, and Bobby understood that she wasn't just giving him news; she expected him to go and look. He was irritated by the casual feminine demand. But temper left him as soon as he was out of the dining-room.

A dim light burned above the stairwell. There was no light in the corridor upstairs. When he put on the light in his room the window threw back a dark reflection. The bed hadn't been turned down; his open suitcase was as he had left it; the yellow native shirt hung on the back of a chair. Nothing had been disturbed; nothing had changed. Only the smells seemed sharper.

He went across the corridor to Linda's room: a smaller room, but lighter and fresher: the colonel had shown Linda favour. On an armchair he saw the brassiere of the day, the shirt, the mud-spattered blue trousers with their intimate creases and still, around the crumpled waistband and smooth hips, retaining something of the shape of the wearer. A bright silver object shone on the bare bedside table: a bit of foil, a sachet torn open by clumsy fingers. It wasn't a shampoo. It was a vaginal deodorant with an appalling name.

The slut, Bobby thought, the slut.

Walking across the dining-room again, he smiled down at the floor. But when he sat down at the table he had stopped smiling and his face was set. He saw that the third place-setting had been cleared away. And again it was a little time before he understood the nature of Linda's stare, which he had been ignoring. He had resolved to be silent; now he found himself saying, in a conspiratorial whisper that matched Linda's, 'I didn't see anyone.'

Linda was less than satisfied. Her forehead twitched; she gave an impatient sigh and shifted away.

Bobby was hating everything.

*

Presently the colonel came in, with his stiff, halting step. He had a finger between the pages of his book. He was flushed;

the gin was working on him. He looked about the room with satisfaction, as though it was quite full. He looked benignly at Linda.

'Have you read this?' He lifted the book: it was by Naomi Jacob: Linda couldn't read the title. 'It's very good about the mentality of the Hun. Don't show me the menu,' he said to the boy. 'I wrote it. I'll have the soup. Used to get them here. Those package tours from Frankfurt. Had to drop them.'

You mean they dropped you, Bobby thought.

'They would eat up your profits,' the colonel said. 'Literally eat them up. We used to do a buffet for them. Terrible idea. Never offer the Hun a buffet. He isn't happy until he's eaten every last scrap. He believes the new ham on the buffet is for him alone. There used to be a stampede. I saw two women fight. No, no; clear away the buffet as soon as you see the Hun coming. Meet the horde at the door and say, "It's strictly fixed portions today, gentlemen."'

'They are tremendous eaters,' Linda said.

'Like the Belgians. Now there's a crowd. We used to get lots of them here from the other side. The only thing you can say for the Belgian is that he knows a good bottle of burgundy. Little of that sort of thing here now, though. Of course a lot of this' – he waved at the wire-netted windows, at the darkness, at the lake – 'a lot of this is their doing. They thought they would just come from little Belgium and start living the good life right away. No work. Nothing like that. Just the good life. There was this woman just before the troubles, she said to me, "But it's our estate. The king gave it to us." You should see what they got up to over there. Mansions, palaces, swimming pools. You should have seen. There's these two tribes among them –'

'The Flemings and the Walloons,' Linda said.

'They sound the opposite of what they should be. The Walloons should be the fat ones, but they are rather thin and refined. The Flemings should be thin, but they are fat. Ever seen a party of Flemings at the trough? They would order dinner for ten o'clock and get here at seven. At *seven*. They would start drinking. Just to make themselves hungry. By eight they would be hungry and nibbling at everything and getting the boys to run back and forth with more and more savouries. You've got to watch the savouries when the Belgians are around. And they would keep on drinking and drinking, getting themselves hungrier and hungrier. The food's in here, the boys are waiting. But they said ten, and they're not coming in until ten. Until ten o'clock they're just building up their appetites. Quarrelling, shouting, playing cards. Children screaming. Everybody shouting at the boys for more savouries. There would be pandemonium in that bar, from one little Fleming family party. Then at ten they would come in and eat solidly for an hour and a half. Grunting and snorting together. Mother, father, child. Everyone a little ball of fat. That was the sort of example they were setting. You can't blame the Africans. The Africans have eyes. They can see. The African's very funny that way. You can drive him hard for weeks on end. But one day he'll gallop away with you.'

There was a crash in the kitchen, and a burst of high-pitched chatter. One voice rose quickly to a squeal which sounded like laughter; and then all the voices in the kitchen squealed together.

The colonel became abstracted; he was no longer looking directly at Linda. The Israelis talked softly. The tall boy came to clear away Bobby and Linda's plates and left a little of his stink behind.

'You saw that chap in the evening dress?' the colonel asked.

Bobby frowned. Linda was about to smile, but she saw that the colonel was not smiling.

'He's been coming here for a month or so. Ever since he picked up those clothes. I don't know who he is.'

Linda said, 'He was awfully polite.'

'Oh yes, all very polite. But he comes to put me in my place, you know. Isn't that so, Timothy?'

The tall boy stood still and raised his head. 'Sir?'

'He would like to kill me, wouldn't he?'

Timothy remained still, the tray in his hands, and tried to look serious. He said nothing. He relaxed only when the colonel went back to his food.

'One day they'll gallop away with you,' the colonel said.

With quick, long strides Timothy went to the kitchen. A fresh voice was added to the squeals there; and then, the voice abruptly withdrawn, an aggrieved squealing going on, Timothy came out again, still brisk, still serious, and went to the table of the Israelis.

'I remember how we'd train men for Salonika, India, and places like that,' the colonel said. 'Sometimes we had to strap them to the horses. *Ah-wa-wa!* You'd hear them bawling at the other end of the ground. Some of them would develop rashes an inch thick. But we'd make riders out of them. We'd get them off to Salonika, India, or wherever it was.' He looked directly at Linda again. 'These names must sound strange to you. I suppose the name of this place will sound strange soon.'

The squealing in the kitchen died down.

The colonel became abstracted again, busy with his food.

A tall, slender African, dark-brown, not black, came out into the dining-room from the kitchen. He moved lightly, like an athlete. He nodded and smiled at the Israelis, at Bobby and Linda, and went to the colonel's table. The mobility and openness of his face made him look less like an African than a West Indian or American mulatto. He wore simple clothes with much style. His well-tailored khaki trousers were clean and ironed; the collar of his grey shirt was clean and firm. His cream-coloured pullover suggested the sportsman, the tennis-player or the cricketer. There was a parting in his hair, and his brown shoes shone.

He stood before the colonel and waited to be seen.

Then he said, 'I come to say good night, sir.' His accent had echoes of the colonel's accent.

'Yes, Peter. You're off. We heard the crash and we heard you squeal. Where to this time?'

'I go cinema, sir.' The pidgin was a surprise.

'You've seen our local bug-house?' the colonel asked Linda. 'I suppose that will close down when the army goes. If the army goes.'

The Israelis didn't hear.

'And what are you going to see, Peter?'

The question confused Peter. He continued to look at the colonel. His face held a half-smile and then went African-blank.

He said, 'I can't remember, sir.'

'That's the African for you,' the colonel said. The words were spoken at Linda but not addressed to her.

Peter waited. But the colonel was occupied with his food. Peter became composed again; the half-smile returned to his face.

He said at last, 'I go, sir?'

The colonel nodded without looking up.

Peter moved away with his light athlete's step. His leather heels sounded on the floor of the bar, the verandah. As soon as they touched the concrete steps, the colonel slammed a sauce bottle down and shouted, *'Peter!'*

Bobby jumped. Timothy held his face straight as though he had just been slapped. Even the Israelis looked up. It was silent in the dining-room, the bar, the kitchen.

Then, as lightly as his leather heels permitted, Peter came back to the dining-room and stood before the colonel's table.

The colonel said, 'Give me the keys for the Volkswagen, Peter.'

'Keys in office, sir.'

'That's a foolish thing to say, Peter. If the keys were in the office, I wouldn't be asking you for them now, would I?'

'No, sir.'

'So it's a foolish thing to say.'

'Foolish thing, sir.'

'So you are very foolish.'

Peter was silent.

'Peter?'

'Foolish thing, sir.'

'Don't say it with so much pride, Peter. If you are foolish, you are foolish and you do foolish things. No witchdoctor is going to cure that.'

Peter no longer glanced about the room; his eyes were fixed on the colonel. His bony shoulders were hunched; he appeared to stoop.

'Oh, he looks so fine,' the colonel said, as though speaking to Linda again; but he wasn't looking at her. 'So polished.' He held out his open palm and raised it up and down. 'Pass by the door of his quarters, and it's all you can do to keep yourself from being sick.'

In his thin face Peter's eyes had begun to stare and shine. His mouth was loose.

'Give me the keys, Peter.'

'Keys in Volkswagen, sir.'

Bobby pushed his plate aside. Linda kicked him below the table. He settled back. The colonel saw. He looked away from Peter to the floor near Bobby's feet, and he seemed to grow abstracted.

He made a gesture with his index finger. 'How wide is the hotel lot, Peter?'

'One hundred and fifty feet, sir.'

'And deep?'

'Two hundred feet.'

'And in those thirty thousand square feet *I* am in charge. I don't care what happens outside. I am in charge here. If you don't like what I do you can get out. Get out at once.'

Bobby pressed a finger on the tablecloth and picked up a crumb.

'What do you think of me, Peter?'

'I like you, sir.'

'He likes me. Peter likes me.'

'You take me in when I was small. You give me job, you give me quarters. You look after my children.'

'He has fourteen. He's living with three of those animals right now. So polished. So nice. So well-spoken. You wouldn't believe he doesn't even know how to hold a pen in those hands. You wouldn't believe the filth he comes out of. But you like dirt, don't you, Peter? You like going in to some black hole to eat filth and dance naked. You will steal and lie to do that, won't you?'

'I like the quarters, sir.'

'While I live you will stay there. You won't move in here, Peter. I don't want you to bank on that. If I die you will starve, Peter. You will go back to bush.'

'That is true, sir.'

'And you like me. I am good to you. But I haven't been good to you. In this room we've had people talking about exterminating you. Don't you remember?'

'I don't remember.'

'You're a liar.'

'I like you, sir.'

'What about the boy who was locked in the refrigerator?'

'That was somewhere else.'

'So you remember that.'

'I never talk about these things, sir.'

'The whippings? There was a lot of that. What about the crops you weren't allowed to grow? You remember that? You say you like me?'

'I hate you, sir.'

'Of course you hate me, and I know you hate me. Last week you killed that South African. Old, helpless. Didn't you? Lived here for twenty years. Married one of your women.'

'Thief kill him, sir.'

'That's what they always say, Peter. But we know who killed him. It was someone who hated him.'

'No, sir.'

'Do you remember when your woman was sick, Peter?'

'You know about that, sir.'

'Tell me again.'

Peter's staring eyes were inflamed, moist with tears of irritation. His half-open mouth was collapsed, the upper part of his face taut.

'It's a story you always tell,' the colonel said. 'People always listen.'

Timothy was leaning against one of the square pillars in the middle of the room, head back, slightly to one side, looking on.

'My wife was sick,' Peter said. He stopped, choked with irritation.

'You had three others. Go on.'

'She cry every night in the quarters.'

'Black with filth and stink.'

'One night she was very sick. I get car and take her to hospital. They say no. Hospital for Eu'peans only. Huts for natives. Indian doctor take her. Too late, sir. She die.'

'And you went out the next day and got other women and sent them to the forest to chop wood. And they loaded up the wood on their backs and came back to you in the evening. It's a good story, especially for visitors.'

'I never talk about these things, sir.'

'Who do you hate more? The Indian or me?'

'I hate the Indian.'

'You are ungrateful. Who do you hate more? The Indian or me?'

'I will always hate you, sir.'

'Don't you forget it. Your hate will keep me alive. One night, Peter, you will knock on my door –'

'No, sir.'

'You will be wearing a raincoat or you will have a jacket. You will be holding your elbows close to your side –'

'No, sir. No, sir.' Peter was closing and opening his eyes.

'I won't behave like the South African, Peter. When you say, "Good evening, sir," I won't say, "Why, it's Peter, my own boy. Come in, Peter. Have some tea. How are you? How's your family?" There'll be no cups of tea. I won't behave like that. I'll be waiting. I'll say, "It's Peter. Peter hates me." And you won't come past that door. I'll kill you. I'll shoot you dead.'

Peter opened his eyes and looked at the top of the colonel's head.

'This is how I swear my oath,' the colonel said. 'Under these lights, in the open, before witnesses. Tell your friends.'

For some time Peter stood looking at the top of the colonel's head. His mouth closed, became firm again; there were no tears in his inflamed eyes. He put his hand in the pocket of his khaki trousers and took out a key-ring with two keys. He was going to place it on the table, but the colonel held out his hand and Peter put the keys in the colonel's palm. There was nothing more to keep him; and with a step as light and springy and athletic as before he walked through the dining-room to the kitchen.

The colonel didn't look at anyone in the room. He took up a glass of water, but his hands trembled and he put the glass down. His face went pale.

Timothy left the pillar and made himself busy.

When the colonel recovered, and colour came back to his face, he looked at Linda and said, 'It's their big night. They've been building up to it all week. Mister Peter was going to turn up in the hotel Volkswagen. A lot of them believe he's already taken over. Oh, out there he's quite a politician, Mister Peter. Well, that's his problem. Isn't it, Timothy?' He had stopped trembling; he smiled at Timothy.

Timothy smiled back, in relief.

There was chatter in the kitchen again. A high-pitched voice began to squeal, and there was laughter.

'Do you hear him?' the colonel said to Linda.

Taking a fork to her mouth, she nodded.

'That's Peter, although you wouldn't believe it. Do you know what they're saying? It sounds as though they're having the most fantastic argument, but they're saying *nothing*. They're like the birds when it comes to chattering. You should hear Timothy here when he gets going.'

Timothy, clearing away the Israelis' last plates, smiled at the compliment, but remained correct. He creased his forehead and pulled back the corners of his closed mouth.

There was a peal of laughter from the kitchen.

'That's Peter all right,' the colonel said. 'They can go on like that for hours. It means nothing at all. What did you think of the dinner?'

'It was very nice,' Linda said.

'Nothing to do with me. Cookboy does it all. Just tells me and I write the menu. You would laugh if you saw him.' The colonel smiled. 'Fresh from the bush. Never sat on a chair until he came here. I wonder what will happen to him when I go. But what's the use?'

'Are you thinking of going?'

'I think of nothing else. But it's too late now. Can't wait for the Americans to come and buy us all out. That'll come. But it'll be too late for me.'

The Israelis, by signs alone, called for their bill. Timothy took their money and gave them change. The colonel made a point of not looking. When the Israelis went past the colonel's table they hesitated and bowed briefly. The colonel said nothing. He raised his eyes to acknowledge them and then he stared into space, as though their passage had disturbed the train of his thoughts. He kept on staring until the Israelis, in the gravelled yard, began to talk more loudly.

'These people don't know how *lucky* they are,' the colonel said.

A car door banged, once, twice. An engine started.

'If the Europeans had come here fifty years earlier, they would have been hunted down like game and exterminated.

Twenty, thirty years later – well, the Arabs would have got here first, and they would all have been roped up and driven down to the coast and sold. That's Africa. They'll kill the king all right. They'll decimate his tribe before this is over. Did you know him? Have you been listening to the news?'

'I only saw him,' Linda said.

'Came here for lunch once. Very polished. If I were a younger man I would go out and try to rescue him. Though that wouldn't have made much sense either. He's no different from the others. Given half the chance, he'd be hunting the witch-doctor. They say there's good and bad everywhere. There's no good and bad here. They're just Africans. They do what they have to do. That's what you have to tell yourself. You can't hate them. You can't even get angry with them. Really angry.'

Dinner was almost over. Timothy was clearing the tables that had been laid and not used.

'Too late,' the colonel said, straightening the magazines and books on his table. 'Too late for that South African. He used to come here, until he had that last stroke. That was his great mistake. A real old Boer. They found the teapot half full, the two cups on the floor, and tea and blood everywhere. Once or twice he brought his wife. The ugliest woman you ever saw. Like a wrinkled and very happy old ape.' He paused. 'These past few years I've seen *things* here that would make you cry.'

At the sudden falseness, the tone of a man saying what he thought was expected of him, Bobby looked up. He saw the colonel looking at him. Bobby, sipping coffee, blew at the steam. The colonel looked away.

The squealing and chatter in the kitchen stopped.

It was like a signal for the colonel. He stood up. 'Not the sort of thing you read in the papers. Not the sort of thing the people in the High Commission want to hear about either. For them it's all sweetness and light now. Mustn't offend the witch-doctor.' Steadying himself on his feet, he straightened the magazines again, rearranged his sauce bottles, took up his book and held it against his chest. 'Not many votes in this quarter now.'

He spoke it like an exit line. Walking off, he held himself exaggeratedly upright, but he couldn't hide his injured hip. In the bar, and then down the verandah to his room, his footsteps were slow, one light, one flat and heavy.

Timothy, moving with a new, almost playful, looseness, swiftly gathered up tablecloths. He made large and rapid gestures; he took long, stretching strides, each ending with a little skid, as though he was demonstrating his great height and reach. His smell swirled about the room.

It was not quite half-past eight.

'I'm beginning to feel there's something to be said for the Belgians,' Linda said. 'Never eat before ten.'

'The Flemings,' Bobby said. 'The fat ones.'

Timothy switched off two of the three lights.

'You are the expert on the local amusements,' Bobby said.

'Wait for me in the bar,' Linda said. 'We might go for a walk.'

Bobby didn't care for her confident, confiding manner. It was as though disappointment, and darkness, had brought out the wife in her and she was casting him in the role of Martin. But he didn't want to be alone either. He went into the bar.

Timothy switched off the last light in the dining-room and could be heard squealing with someone in the kitchen. The barboy was behind the bar, still drooping, still apparently studying the bar; it turned out now that he was reading a book. Presently Linda came down, a cardigan hanging on her shoulders. She gave a comic shiver, as though shivering at more than cold.

*

In the boulevard they couldn't hear the voices from the kitchen or the quarters. They heard only the sound of their shoes on the sand and loose gravel of the broken road and the occasional slap of the unseen lake against the lake wall. The glow from the quarters at the back gave depth to the hotel building; the light from the bar, spreading out into the yard on one side, and show-ing faintly through the open windows of the unlit dining-room on the other side, outlined the hotel's concrete wall. Beyond that was the darkness of the great tree and the empty house.

Linda said, 'I wouldn't like to be by myself here.'

Ahead of them was one of the street lamps that worked, a splintering, fluorescent circle, smoky after the day's rain. Objects began to define themselves; shadows grew hard. Light fell on the stepped line of a broken brick wall. Wet palm fronds shone; there were glitters in the park.

'It's funny,' Linda whispered, 'how you can forget the houses and feel that the lake hasn't even been discovered.'

'I don't know what you mean by discovered,' Bobby said, not whispering. 'The people here knew about it all the time.'

'I've heard that one. I just wish they'd managed to let the rest of us know.'

They came to the house with the broken corrugated-iron roof that hung down like a bird's spread wing. In the verandah there was a group squatting around a small fire.

Linda said, 'They hadn't moved into the boulevard when I was here the last time.'

As she spoke, she stumbled. A pebble skidded away. An African stood up in the verandah, thin bare legs and ragged jacket silhouetted against the fire. Linda and Bobby looked straight ahead.

When they had passed the house, Linda said, 'He's right. They'll kill him.'

They passed the filling station; the tourist shop; the cinema, still blank and closed. They came to the end of the boulevard and continued into the tree-hung lane from which the running soldiers had come out earlier that evening. There was no asphalt surface on this lane; their feet fell on wet sand, pebbles, leaves. The blackness grew intense very quickly. The pale walls of villas set far back in gloomy overgrown gardens were barely visible; verandahs were like part of the surrounding blackness. There were no fires here. The trees were low above the lane; the sense of openness had gone.

A dog barked, a low, deep sound; and then it was beside them, big and growling. They walked on, the dog shepherding them angrily past his lot. Dogs barked on either side of the road ahead. And soon they were walking between dogs that obeyed no boundaries. A faint electric light, not a campfire, burned in an inside room of a villa. From that villa, too, dogs came bounding, without a bark, paws ripping through undergrowth and then, over the low twisted wooden fence, beating lightly on the sand of the road, scattering small pebbles. And always, from the black road ahead, came the sound of more dogs. No voices called to the dogs.

'This is nonsense,' Linda said.

They turned back. But where before the dogs had only been keeping them to the centre of the lane, now the dogs crossed in front of them and behind them. Paws pattered on the sand and made an almost metallic sound; growls were deep, abrupt, never loud. Always there was barking in the distance. The pack grew.

'Oh my God,' Linda said. 'These dogs don't have any owners. They've gone wild.'

'Don't *talk*,' Bobby said. 'And for God's sake don't stumble.'

And their speech did madden the dogs more. Now the dogs occupied the lane completely and their movements were thick and flurried. They were waiting for a signal: the first leap by the bravest in the pack, a sudden gesture from Bobby or Linda, a dislodged pebble. But, steadily, the boulevard and the light came nearer.

'You said your mother's dog left those two parallel lines on your calf?' Linda said.

Rage overcame Bobby. 'I'll kill them. I'm wearing these steel-tipped shoes. I'll kill the first one that attacks me. I'll kick its skull in. I'll kill it.'

The anger stayed with him and was like courage. And it was as if the dogs responded to his anger. They began to keep to the edge of the lane; they began to fall behind. But the boulevard was near; the darkness was thinning in the fluorescent light; and the boulevard was the boundary the dogs recognized.

Bobby was trembling. Slowly on the boulevard the sense of time came back to him.

Linda was saying, 'They say you have to have fourteen injections for tetanus.'

'They brought these dogs here to attack Africans.'

'All right, Bobby. They're attacking everybody now.'

'They trained them to attack Africans.'

'They didn't train them very well.'

'It isn't funny.'

'How do you think I feel?'

They walked back to the hotel without talking. They didn't look at the campfires they passed. In the hotel the bar lights were still on; there was no light in the colonel's room, next to the office. In the verandah Linda appeared to wait for Bobby to say something. He said nothing. He set his face, turned away from her, and went alone into the bar. She went down the verandah to the passage; he heard her go up the stairs to her room. It was just past nine. The adventure had lasted less than half an hour.

*

Bobby sat on a barstool and drank Dubonnet. The fear drained out of him; the moment of panic in the dark lane became remote. The anger turned to exhaustion, and melancholy at his own solitude, in that bar, beside that vast African lake. Vacantly considering the dusty head of the barboy in the red tunic,

Bobby thought: poor boy, poor African, poor African's head; and tears began to come to Bobby's eyes.

'I read French book,' the barboy said, showing a tattered book in very limp covers.

Bobby heard but didn't understand. He looked at the boy and remembered the dogs and thought: poor boy.

'I read geometry,' the barboy said, lifting another tattered book from below the bar.

And Bobby understood that the barboy was trying to start a conversation. It was what some young Africans did. They tried to start conversations with people they thought were visitors and kindly; they hoped not only to practise their English but also to acquire manners and knowledge. It moved Bobby to be singled out in this way; it moved him that, after all that had happened, the boy should show such trust; and it distressed him that he had allowed himself to be influenced by the colonel and had so far not looked at the boy, had seen only an African in uniform, one of the colonel's employees, part of the hateful hotel.

'You read geometry,' Bobby said. 'You show me where you read.'

The barboy smiled and danced up and down on his toes. He pressed his elbows on the bar and at the same time turned the first few pages of the book, gathering up each page with the whole of his palm. The pages he turned were black and furred, the edges worn.

'I read here,' the boy said. Still hopping, he placed a palm across two pages and shoved the book towards Bobby.

Bobby put the book in the middle of the bar. 'You read here?

The three angles of a triangle together make one hundred and eighty degrees?'

'I read here.' The boy leaned sideways across the bar. 'You teach me.'

'I teach you. You give me paper.'

The boy brought out a chit-pad.

'Look, I teach you. I draw straight line. That straight line make one hundred and eighty degrees. Hundred eighty. Look now. I draw triangle on straight line. Like that. That angle here and that other angle here and that angle up there, all that make hundred eighty degrees. You understand?'

'Hundate.'

'You no understand. Look, I teach you again. I draw circle here. Circle make three hundred and sixty degrees.'

'Hundate.'

'No. No hundate. Three hundred and sixty. Three hundan-sixty. I show you hundate. I draw line through circle. Hundate up there. Hundate here.'

'I read French.'

'You read plenty. What for you like read so much?'

'I go school next year,' the boy said, showing off now, looking down his nose, sticking out his lower lip, and pulling back the geometry book with the fingertips of both hands. 'I buy more schoolbooks. I get big job.'

The words had echoes: Bobby understood that someone must have passed this way before. Adventure was not in Bobby's mind; adventure was what he had ceased to hope for that day. But now, with sadness for the boy who might have had a previous teacher, he saw that adventure was coming; and, as so often, it was coming when it was least expected, so that it seemed just, like reward. Teaching the boy, he had not studied him. Now he looked at the boy's head, dust adhering to oil; he looked at the lean, tough neck. And the boy, knowing he was being appraised, looked down gravely at his French book, moving his swollen lips.

'What's your name?' Bobby asked, looking at the boy's ears.

'Carolus.' The boy didn't look up.

'You have nice name.'

'You teach me French.'

The French grammar, its limp red cloth cover stained and sticky and bleached and curling, had been written by an Irish priest and printed in Ireland.

'How far you reach? You reach here? Partitive article?'

'Partitive.'

'In English you no have partitive article. You no say, "Bring me some ink."' Bobby paused: language teaching had unexpected difficulties. 'In French you always say, "Bring me *some* ink."'

'*Some* ink.'

'That's it.'

Bobby looked at the boy, and the boy looked down at the book and moved a thick tongue slowly between his lips.

'What time bar close?' Bobby said.

'You teach me *English*,' the boy said. 'You no teach me French. You no know French?'

'I know French. Look, I teach you. In English you say ink.'

'Ink.'

'In French you say *l'encre*.'

'Link.'

'What time bar close?'

'Any time. Link. You teach me more.'

'Bring me some ink. Bring me *de l'encre*. *De l'encre*. How you mean, any time?'

The boy went coy. He hung his head low over the disintegrating Irish book, so that Bobby saw the top of his head: particles of fluff trapped between the springs.

'Bar close ten o'clock,' the boy said.

'You bring me tea ten o'clock.'

The boy hung his head lower. 'Kitchen close.'

'You bring me tea. Room four. I teach you more.' Bobby folded the fingers of his hand and rubbed his knuckles through the oily springs of the barboy's hair. 'I give you shilling.'

'Kitchen close,' the boy said.

Bobby placed his palm on the boy's taut neck, half on the springy hair, half on the warm skin. 'What a little bargainer it is,' he said; and, suddenly pulling the boy's face across the bar to his own, he whispered into his ear, 'I give you five.'

The boy didn't pull his head back and Bobby, still holding the boy's head close and feeling the boy straining to be still, began rubbing his thumb behind the boy's left ear, feeling the bone below the smooth African skin. The boy became very quiet. Tears came to Bobby's eyes; and though he was looking at his own thumb and the intricate modelling of the boy's ear and the coarse little springs of hair, he was not thinking of the boy or the dogs or the intimacies to come; he was surrendering only to his own tenderness and melancholy, which at such moments overflowed.

Suddenly the boy jumped away.

The burglar alarm on Bobby's car was shrieking. The sharp metallic vibrations rose and fell around a central, persistent wail. The hotel yard jumped with light, bright bulb after bright bulb, everywhere. The quarters broke out into high-pitched chatter, which instantly developed into a general squealing.

'Peter!' the colonel called. 'Peter!'

From the quarters women wailed. Footsteps were everywhere, in the yard, in the hotel itself.

The boy was looking at Bobby with eyes of terror.

The burglar alarm continued to shriek. It would not subside until the car ceased to rock and became still again.

'Peter!' the colonel called.

Bobby went out to the verandah. The colonel's room at the end of the verandah was lit up. The door was open; the window at the back of the room showed the brightly lit yard.

The garage was an open shed. A naked bulb burned there now and threw deep shadows. The rocking of the car was not perceptible, but the alarm was still going, the central wail broken.

Bobby saw that no wheel was missing from his car, no hubcap taken off.

The silences between the wails grew longer, the wail itself fainter. The alarm became a series of cheeps, pips, and then finally died. And then the brightness of the awakened yard was as startling as the alarm had been.

Bobby went back to the bar. The boy still looked at him with eyes of terror. He had put on all the bar lights.

'Peter,' the colonel was saying.

At last the quarters went quiet.

'Dog or cat jump on car, sir.'

'Were you sleeping?'

'Sleeping, sir.'

'You are very foolish.'

Women wailed.

'I'm going to have you tied up. Timothy! Carolus!'

The barboy jerked his head. But he didn't move.

The wailing continued, drowning the colonel's questions, the soft responses.

'Carolus!'

Now Carolus moved. His mouth, half open, had grown thick and immobile. His movement was awkward, his limbs heavy. He opened the back door of the bar and stood for a little with his back to Bobby, his hand behind him on the doorknob. Across the dark wide passageway half a panelled door was ajar, and Bobby had a glimpse of the bright yard: the unshaded bulbs on the cylindrical metal legs of the water-tower, the glare of the white-washed quarters, the bush at the back that glittered in black shadow and looked artificial.

'Carolus!'

He pulled the door shut, and Bobby was alone in the bar. With all the lights on it seemed a bigger room.

Outside, the women wailed in relay, no two drawing breath at the same time. It was impossible to pick out what the male voices were saying. The wailing became simple sound, part of the background.

In a framed signed photograph behind the bar, the photograph enlarged, imprecise, a man in a boat held up a big fish and smiled in strong sunlight: the weather and the mood, and all the implied order, of a particular day. There was a calendar, with an African landscape, from a Belgian brewery, the names of towns in Belgium and Africa printed in the same red type. The paint on the half-empty shelves was old and scratched, cream below brown; in one corner half a dozen nearly empty liqueur bottles had old, dry, stained labels.

The wailing outside grew weaker, was no longer background. Bobby heard the colonel's voice. The wailing grew loud again, subsided again, and then there was almost silence.

Bobby left the bar and went quickly down the verandah to the enclosed passageway. The door that gave on to the yard was ajar. He didn't look. He was aware of brightness, movement. He also knew he had been observed.

Upstairs, as he was opening his door, he heard Linda open hers. She was in a short cotton nightdress; her shiny shins looked as sharp as her elbows.

She whispered, 'Peter? I knew it, I knew it.'

Again he felt that she was involving him in a neutral marital intimacy. And though he half wanted the company, he was perverse. He set his face, as though he had been especially affronted by what had happened downstairs, turned away from Linda and without a word pushed his door open.

It was unexpectedly bright with the glare from the yard. He closed the door, deciding at the last moment to give a little slam. He kicked something across the floor. He didn't need to turn on the light to see that it was the key of his car.

*

It was only when he was undressed that he became disquieted. Intruders: there might have been a crisis, and he might have been without his car, trapped. He decided then to pack, to be ready at any time for a swift getaway. He arranged, around a chair, everything he would need: packed suitcase, trousers, the yellow native shirt, shoes and socks. He went to bed in his vest and underpants. It was pointless, even a little deranged; it was the behaviour of the compound. But when the lights in the yard went off, and he felt himself alone in the darkness, he was glad he had done what he had done.

There was a knock on the door, but so gentle he couldn't be sure. He waited. The knock came again. He sat up; he didn't put the light on. The door opened, the ceiling light was turned on. It wasn't Linda. It was Carolus, with a tea-tray. The world was normal again; the hotel was the hotel.

'You close door,' Bobby said.

Carolus closed the door.

'You bring tea, Carolus? You very good boy. You bring tea here.'

Carolus set the tray on the bedside table. Just as his limbs had lost their lightness, and he moved clumsily, so his face had altered. His eyes had gone red, his lips thick, creased and dry, with a white bloom; his whole face appeared inflamed with apprehension and mistrust.

'You sit here. You talk with me. I teach you.'

Carolus was taking out a piece of paper from the tight pocket of his red tunic.

'I teach you French? I teach you hundate?'

The paper was a chit for the tea. It was made out in soft pencil, in the colonel's firm handwriting.

Anger swept through Bobby; and his anger grew at the sight of Carolus's heavy face.

He ordered: 'Pencil.'

Carolus had one waiting.

'Now get out!' Bobby said, handing back the pencil and the chit.

Carolus didn't move. His expression didn't alter.

'Go!'

'You give me.'

'Give you? Give you nothing. Give you whip.'

It wasn't even true; it was someone else's words; he was violating himself. Sitting up in bed, looking at the inflamed African face coming nearer to his, he saw it invaded by such blank and mindless rage that his own anger vanished in terror, terror at something he sensed to be beyond his control, beyond his reason.

He said, 'I give you. I promise you. I give you.'

He took up a shilling from the change he had put out on the bedside table.

'You give me five.'

'I give you, I give you.'

Even when he had the money, Carolus looked at it suspiciously, and then he looked from his palm to Bobby's face. And as soon as Carolus began to walk to the door Bobby understood that Carolus was only 'fresh from the bush'; and Bobby knew that he had misread the boy's face, had seen things in it that were not there.

He said, 'Boy.'

Carolus stopped. He started to turn to face Bobby.

'You take off light, boy.'

Carolus obeyed. And when he left the room he shut the door quietly behind him.

Bobby turned on the bedside lamp. He poured a cup of tea. It was weak and full of leaves; it had been brewed in water that was barely hot. It was awful.

7

HE WAS IN A CAR with a woman whose identity he couldn't be sure of. They were quarrelling. Everything she said was accurate; everything was wounding; and though to everything there was a reply, he couldn't explain himself. He had to shout above her shouts; he was screaming; and as they sped along the empty road, dangerously, the wheel jumping in his hands, she wounded him and wounded him, more and more deeply; and there was rage and ache in his head, which seemed about to explode. He was no longer in the car. He was standing beside a table in a room full of people and chatter; and his exploding head made him collapse and stretch out right there, before them, on the floor.

When he awoke there was only the memory of the head. The woman and her arguments had vanished; but the wound remained. It was dark, but there was a quality about the darkness which suggested that it would soon be light. He reasoned: it was his early night, the events of the evening, and anyway he had packed for a quick getaway. Just the trousers and the native shirt, and he would be off. But petrol: he didn't have enough, his tank wasn't filled: again and again he panicked as in his dream. And then it was daylight: a faint chattering from the quarters, a glimpse of trees at the back which he hadn't seen the previous evening, and the radio downstairs, the African announcer stumbling over the violent words of the news bulletin from the capital.

It was the light, the openness, the lake, that surprised him when he went down to the dining-room. The sky was high and blue; beyond the ornamental palms on the boulevard the lake stretched to the horizon. The previous evening the wire-netting on the dining-room windows had appeared to enclose the room; now it offered no barrier to the light and was scarcely visible. So sodden and heavy and gloomily tropical the previous evening; but now the air was fresh. The hotel, the boulevard, the park, the lake: something of the resort atmosphere survived. And this morning there was activity on the boulevard. Above the hotel's concrete wall an army lorry could be seen moving slowly from left to right.

The colonel, dressed as before, was at his table. He had almost finished breakfast; he was drinking tea and reading his book. Bobby, in his yellow native shirt, forgot about the lake and the light; and, left hand at his side, right hand swinging, made his swift, grim passage to the only other table that had been laid. Seated, his face set, he looked at the colonel; but the colonel was reading. Crumbs on the tablecloth, disorder in the butter-flecked marmalade: Linda had been down already. Grimly, Bobby buttered a piece of cold toast.

'News not so good this morning,' the colonel said. His voice was relaxed and casual. 'Still, I suppose the sooner this thing's over the better for all of us.'

Bobby, biting on his hard toast, gave a brief, blank smile. The colonel didn't see; he was turning the page of his book.

Timothy, his smell sharp in the light morning air, offered the breakfast card. The card was as dingy as the red-checked waiter's rag Timothy flicked about the table. His gestures were freer this morning. He was almost skittish, almost familiar, and he appeared anxious to talk. With every friendly flick of his rag he released a little more of his smell.

Another lorry went grinding past the hotel.

'Army's on the move this morning,' the colonel said. 'Not a time to be on the road, when our army's on the move. I always give them a wide berth myself.'

'I imagine the road's still wet,' Bobby said.

'Oh, one or two of those lorries are going to come to grief down some precipice or the other.'

The colonel smiled directly at Bobby. The colonel looked older this morning; but there was no strain in his face; the flesh around his eyes and mouth looked softer and rested.

Bobby was uncertain about the joke.

The colonel noticed. 'They're going to leave the road in an awful state.'

'But I imagine it'll dry out pretty quickly,' Bobby said. 'With this sun.'

'Oh, with this sun it'll dry out in no time at all. No time at all. By lunchtime, I'd say.'

It was like an invitation to linger; it was unexpected. But Linda had been down; she and the colonel had no doubt talked.

A car came into the yard. A door slammed. The colonel put a marker, a polished strip of bamboo shaped like a paper-knife, clearly an old possession, in his book; and waited. He appeared to know who the visitor was.

It was Peter, coming in from the bar with his light athletic steps. He was in khaki this morning: the khaki trousers of the previous evening, an ironed khaki shirt with epaulettes and button-down pockets. His sleeves were rolled up; there was a big wristwatch with a shining stainless-steel strap on his left wrist. His arms were bony, the muscles slack; the crinkled loose skin around his elbows showed that he was older than he looked. He carried two or three handwritten lists; he must have been out shopping.

When he saw Bobby, Peter paused, bowed and smiled and said in his English accent, 'Good morning, sir.'

There was no irony in the smile. It was like the smile of an old acquaintance. It didn't go with the bow; it was part of Peter's disjointedness. Like his clothes, like the bow, like the accent, Peter's smile was only one part of his training, and it was separate from the other parts. Like Carolus and Timothy, Peter belonged to the hotel and the boys' quarters of the hotel. It was disturbing; as always in former settler haunts, Bobby felt he was trespassing.

Peter stood easily by the colonel's table while the colonel went through the lists. When Peter went away, after bowing again to Bobby and smiling, the colonel stood up, holding his book against his chest. He steadied himself and threw back his shoulders. Then he hesitated, as though listening to the whine of the army lorry on the boulevard.

He smiled at Bobby and said, 'At times like this I always feel that the nearer you are to an army camp the safer it is. They're more under control. I don't know whether you were here for the mutiny. Even the witchdoctor ran away. Nobody knew where he was for a week. But it was perfectly all right here.'

Again Bobby was uncertain.

'Of course it'll all blow over in a day or two,' the colonel said. 'Everybody'll be calmer. Day or two.'

Bobby wasn't sure, but he thought the colonel was asking for company. He said, 'We're a day late as it is.'

'We'll give you an early lunch. You'll get to the Collectorate well before the curfew.'

'So that's official, the curfew?'

'Four o'clock. We'll get you off in good time.'

*

Later Bobby came downstairs to find Linda in the verandah. She was looking at the bright lake through her dark glasses. She had changed her shirt but was wearing yesterday's blue trousers; there were faint dusty stains where the mud had been brushed off.

She said, 'Has the colonel told you?'

She moved away without waiting for his reply. They were still quarrelling.

Bobby was in no mood to talk; he especially wished to be spared the colonel's disquieting company; and he decided, with relief, to go grim. Grim-faced, he looked through the paperbacks in the office, war stories, historical romances; made a selection; and settled down in a red-painted wicker chair in the verandah to a sulky read.

Linda attached herself to the colonel. They sat in the open office and Bobby heard the colonel talking. They walked about the yard, the garage, the garden, the quarters, and Bobby heard the colonel talking. They sat in the colonel's open room; they came out and stood in the hotel gateway. The colonel appeared to recognize this gateway as a boundary. He kept within the gravelled yard and never stepped on the concrete that sloped down to the asphalt of the boulevard.

At intervals the army lorries rolled slowly by. Below green forage caps the fat faces of the soldiers were expressionless and still matt-black from their morning wash.

The air lost its morning freshness; the light became hard; and Bobby, not held by the paperbacks, began again to feel something of the desolation of the derelict resort. Carolus came into the bar, dusty-headed, oily-skinned, in his old black trousers and tight red tunic, as though he hadn't taken off his clothes or washed since the previous evening. He moved noisily about the bar with broom and rag, taking long, skidding steps, as if in imitation of Timothy. Then he saw Bobby in the verandah. Carolus didn't come out to the verandah. He retreated with his broom and rag and stayed in the bar, out of sight. Bobby didn't move. He put his book face down on his knees, looked at a point in the yard, and frowned. He heard Carolus moving quietly in the bar, trying not to draw attention to himself.

The colonel and Linda were still together, but there were now passages of silence between them. When they came and sat at Bobby's table, for coffee, Bobby saw that they had done so because they had exhausted the mood that had been created by their conversation.

Bobby, still grim, made no effort to talk. Neither did Linda, half smiling behind her dark glasses. And the colonel seemed to have nothing more to say.

Bobby thought: he'll start talking about Africans.

Carolus stood in a doorway with the coffee-tray.

The colonel said, 'It looks as though the lorries have stopped.'

Bobby looked at Carolus and then stared into space, demonstrating his capacity for sternness, even in the colonel's company Carolus became quite stupid and heavy with fright.

'What gets me, you know,' the colonel said, setting out the cups with his firm, square hands, 'is the way those Africans manage to look so downtrodden as soon as they're obeying orders. Did you see those drivers? Driving very, very slowly, and looking very, very downtrodden, as though they'd all had the rod this morning. It's only because those instructors are looking on.'

Bobby, not talking, tilted his empty cup to study a flaw in the glazing.

'You can train them so far and so far only,' the colonel said, taking the cup from Bobby. 'Carolus. Soon they are going to be driving those lorries like madmen, and those same downtrodden faces are going to look very nasty. Carolus.'

Carolus was standing in the doorway, looking in terror from Bobby to the colonel.

Bobby stared at Carolus.

'Carolus,' the colonel said, irritation breaking into his voice for the first time that morning, 'this cup is absolutely filthy.'

Carolus brought another cup. They had coffee. But the colonel's irritation, which had at first seemed only assumed, remained. The calm of the morning had gone; his face was becoming strained again. Linda was silent, smiling behind her dark glasses, as if with inner content. Bobby continued to be grim.

After coffee the colonel left them. And though they heard him talking to the kitchen about their lunch, he behaved afterwards as though they had already left. He didn't come to the bar or the dining-room while they were having their lunch. Timothy, his own manner less skittish now, brought their bill and took their money.

The colonel was in the yard when Bobby and Linda came down with their suitcases, but he didn't appear to see. He didn't appear to hear when Bobby unlocked the car door and the burglar alarm brayed. Hands in pockets, the colonel stood in the gateway. He looked at the boulevard and the lake; sometimes he looked at the hotel building, remotely, as though considering a picture. He didn't hear the car start; he didn't notice it coming close. But suddenly, as Bobby slowed down, the colonel leaned forward and smiled at Linda.

He said, 'If you run into the army, play dead.'

As Bobby moved off, a group of eight men began coming up to the yard from the boulevard. Two were Indians in turbans; the others were young Africans in white shirts and dark trousers, trainee-surveyors perhaps, builders from the army camp, or employees of the Works Department. One of the Indians spoke to the colonel.

'*Lunch!*' the colonel shouted. 'This isn't a roadhouse. You can't just walk in here at any hour you choose and demand *lunch*.'

Down the concrete incline, Bobby and Linda turned into the boulevard, whose ruin, in daylight, the colours so bright, so new, startled them afresh. The thin asphalt surfacing was swollen and cracked like the crust on a cake.

'No!' the colonel was shouting. 'No! No!'

'That was for your benefit,' Bobby said to Linda. 'You made a great hit there.'

'Oh dear. He could do with the money too. Eight fifteens, that's a hundred and twenty shillings. Not counting the drinks.'

'I shouldn't worry. They'll get their lunch. Shall we come back and check, after we get our petrol?'

She lifted her chin, gave an impatient little sniff, and turned to look at the green damp walls of the empty house which the previous evening she hadn't been able to see.

8

THE PETROL STATION worked. They got their petrol; that
secret anxiety of Bobby's was stilled. To avoid passing in front
of the hotel again, he turned down a side street and drove out of
the resort by a street that ran parallel to the lake boulevard.
Soon the scattered villas on the edge of the town were left
behind, and they were on the mountain road.

The soft shoulders of the road had been churned up by the
army lorries, but the central surface was firm and dry. Here and
there, especially at corners, rain and the lorries had dislodged
rocks and created muddy potholes; in some places, where the
road had subsided, large rocks stuck out; but the road was gen-
erally easy. The road-menders hadn't been at work on this side
of the resort; no one had dumped mounds of earth.

They climbed higher. They entered forest, still wet, with
soft spots of sunshine on the road and the dark tangled hillsides.
The light and openness of the lake were shut out. Sometimes
they had a view of the lake below them, no longer glittering,
indistinguishable from the sky; and when they came out of the

forest into the damp valleys of ferns and bamboos the sky seemed lower and more oppressive, and the light had a different quality, settled, dead, holding no reflection from a water surface.

They hadn't been talking.

Now Linda said, 'You wonder how they ever managed to find the place.'

She was being provocative; their quarrel was still on. Bobby didn't reply, and she said nothing else. After some time she carefully changed her position in her seat.

Bamboos and ferns dropped away. At the top of the ridge the land was quite bare. Then they began to go down again, past a valley which was like the valleys they had seen the day before. Again there were fields, terraced hills, huts. In the rain the day before the colours had been soft, green and grey; the paths had meandered into mist; the fields had been empty. Now in the dead sunlight the colours were harsher. Mud was black, vegetation was shining green. The huts that yesterday in the rain had looked such comforting shelters were now seen to be rough structures of grass standing in fenced yards of trampled black mud. Women and children in bright clothes were at work with simple implements in little patches of wet black earth. The women maintained a fixed stoop on straight, firm legs, their broad hips rigid, exaggeratedly humped; so, doubled up, flexible and curving only from waist to head, they hoed and weeded and stepped along their row. All over the valley, among the women and the children, there were little smoking bonfires of damp weedings. It was the immemorial

life of the forest. The paths were simple forest paths, leading
to nothing else.

At a twist in the road ahead, where the bare verge widened
and rose and fell away, half a dozen small domestic animals
stood together silhouetted against the sky. But two turned out
to be naked children. Dull-eyed, disfigured with mud, they
stood where they were and watched the car pass.

Linda said, 'I was hoping to buy some of those White
Fathers cigars for Martin. Do you know them? You could get a
great big bundle for a few shillings. Wrapped in a sort of dry
banana-leaf box.'

Martin, Bobby thought: they were getting near home. He
said, 'I thought Martin was a pipe man.'

'He loves these. They're absolutely vile, but he likes to puff
away and fill his room with the smoke. Just puffing away. Into
curtains, bookshelves, under cushions. Just to get the smell
everywhere. You used to be able to get them at the colonel's.
But I didn't see them this time, and I forgot to ask. I imagine
they used to come from the other side of the lake. But I suppose the poor old White Fathers now have other things to think
about instead of cigars.'

'I don't know. I wonder why we always think when things
are not going well for us that it's all coming to an end.'

'The colonel's under no illusion on that score. Oh dear, it
was awful.'

'I'm in no position to judge,' Bobby said. 'I've never been
one for settler grandeur.'

'It's gone down so much. I suppose since he had that accident and damaged his hip. The rooms are so awful and the boys are so dirty, and he's stopped looking after himself.'

'"That's what happens the minute you take your eyes off them."'

Linda missed the irony. Her silence was like simple agreement.

Bobby tried again. 'I thought only Africans smelled. What is it that Doris Marshall says? That little bit of settler wisdom about civilization and cleanliness?'

'Oh goodness,' Linda said. 'That Timothy.'

Bobby let the subject drop.

Linda said, 'I suppose there must be hundreds of people like that all over the world, in all sorts of strange places.'

'They've had a good life.'

'That's not the point.'

'What is?'

'I don't believe you want to understand. It's so awful.' Her voice broke; it took Bobby by surprise. 'The foolish man is trying to live on his will alone. Oh dear. And the shirt he was wearing was so dirty. He wanted the company. And he's right. They're waiting to kill him.'

'I'd kill him myself if I stayed there.'

'I don't trust that Peter one little bit. A little too fawning and smooth, with that fancy wristwatch.'

Bobby said, 'Peter is a little too clean, I must admit.'

'The colonel was shell-shocked in the Great War. He told me. He said that if anyone scolded him he became unconscious. Scolded, that was the word he used. Then he said he pulled himself together.'

Bobby suppressed his unease. 'He can go South.' He paused. 'Still a lot of blacks there he can take it out of.'

'If you put it like that. But it doesn't matter where he goes now. He took Peter in as a boy, fresh from the bush –'

'– and trained him. I know.'

'I suppose they had a good life, as you say. But what strange places they landed themselves in. Salonika, India.'

'How quickly we pick things up. I wasn't aware that we sent settlers to Salonika.'

'I don't even know where Salonika is. He's sick of the sight of the lake, sick of the hotel and the quarters, sick of his own food and the table he goes to three times a day. But he won't leave. He told me he hadn't been outside his gate for months.'

'That doesn't sound like will to me. I used to have an aunt like that, in darkest England.'

'And he's still so damned fair. He still gives you a five-course dinner.'

She had been talking slowly; he thought she was only growing 'mystical'. But then he saw a thin trickle of tears below her dark glasses. He wanted to say: I know why you're crying. But he decided to let her be, to do nothing that would feed her mood.

He concentrated on his driving. Always, on the rocky road, there were signs of the army lorries that had gone before: the churned-up soft edges, massively embossed with tyre-treads, the muddy potholes at some corners, and occasionally a dislodged boulder, white where it had been buried, earth colour above that. The road continued to be reasonably easy, and empty.

'I suppose you're right,' Linda said. 'Let the dead bury the dead.'

*

Valley led to valley. The road climbed and dropped. But they kept going lower. The valleys became wider; the earth became less black, rockier; the light became more tropical. The dwellings were no longer all of grass; not all had fences and trampled yards. There were little clusters of timber-and-corrugated-iron shacks; and sometimes now there were even ruins, of weathered boards and rusting corrugated iron.

Something like a monument appeared beside the road. It looked like a war memorial or a drinking fountain. It turned out to be a standpipe: a black nozzle sticking out of a large concrete wall with bevelled edges and cut-away corners, PUBLIC WORKS AND WELFARE JOINT ADMINISTRATION 27–5–54 roughly picked out in a stripe of blue-and-white mosaic at the top of the wall. It was the first of eight monumental standpipes. Then once more there was only the road.

From the car they had intermittent glimpses of a rocky river, widening as the land grew flatter. And then the road came out from a cutting in the bush and ran on a high concrete-walled embankment beside the sprawling riverbed: narrow muddy channels between islands of sand and half-stripped shrubs and heaped rocks white in the sunlight. There was no barrier on the embankment, and the openness gave a sense of hazard.

The road turned away from the river and entered bush again. But the river remained close; and when the road next twisted down out of the bush, to run beside the river once more, Bobby and Linda saw a soldier in a crimson beret standing in bright sunlight on the wide concrete wall of the embankment, the khaki of his uniform and the shining black of his face, contrasting textures, clear and sharp against the openness of the riverbed.

He waved at the car, leaning forward slightly, keeping his polished black boots together. African labourers in the valleys were thin, their clothes ragged. The soldier's ironed uniform was tight over his round arms and thighs and his soldier's paunch. He was conscious of his difference, of the army clothes, the evidence of the army diet. His wave was heavy and awkward and looked frantic, but it held authority; and there was confidence in the round, smiling face.

Bobby was driving slowly on the rocky road.

Linda said, 'He's a nice fat one.'

The African continued to smile and wave, his hand flapping from the wrist. The car didn't stop. The African's hand dropped; his face went blank.

Bobby, glancing at the shaking rear-view mirror, had a momentary, confused sense of openness and hazard: the barrierless high embankment tilting behind him, racing beside him. He looked down from the mirror to the road.

'I don't like that look he gave us,' Linda said. 'Now I imagine he's going to telephone his other fat friends, and they'll be waiting for us at some roadblock. I imagine he's running to beat out the message on his drums right at this moment.'

'I always give Africans lifts.'

'I didn't stop you.'

'How do you mean, you didn't stop me?'

'Just what I said. They'll pick you out anywhere, in that yellow native shirt.'

'For God's sake.'

He had been slowing down. Now, a little too wildly, he accelerated.

'I suppose it's because they can't read,' Linda said, 'but they're very sharp. You know that sort of common near the compound. Martin and I were driving past that one day, when we saw Doris Marshall's houseboy, or steward, I suppose we should say, rolling about on the grass, dead drunk as usual, in the middle of the afternoon. As soon as he saw us he ran out right into the road to wave us down. Martin was for stopping. I wasn't. Well, that drunken houseboy *saw* that conversation from fifty or a hundred feet away, and repeated it word for word to Doris Marshall. Doris didn't like it. Suffafrican ittykit. I'd wounded her steward's feelings.'

Bobby braked. When the car stopped he held the steering-wheel hard and leaned over it.

'Oh, Bobby. I wasn't being serious.'

He closed his eyes, then opened them.

'Really, I wasn't being serious. You weren't thinking of going back for him?'

It was, vaguely, what he had in mind.

'That would be too ridiculous.'

'I knew there was something I should have done this morning,' Bobby said. 'I should have telephoned Ogguna Wanga-Butere or Busoga-Kesoro. It's just occurred to me.'

She accepted the explanation. 'I doubt whether either of them's at work today.'

Bobby put his hand to the ignition switch.

In the distance, from the direction of the plain, there was the sound of a helicopter. It was a faint sound, now coming on the wind, now vanishing, then at last steady. When Bobby turned on the ignition, the helicopter couldn't be heard.

*

They drove towards the plain and the sound of the helicopter, approaching, receding, always audible above the beat of the engine and the rattle of the car on the rocky road. They lost the river; but all the land now had the bleached quality of a riverbed. There were a few scattered huts on stilts. Cactus bloomed and threw black shadows. The road became sand, with sunken wheel-tracks; at corners there were drifts of dry loose sand in which the car wheels slipped. It was an old, exhausted land. But it was inhabited.

Two men ran out into the road. But perhaps they were only boys. They were naked, and chalked white from head to toe, white as the rocks, white as the knotted, scaly lower half of the tall cactus plants, white as the dead branches of trees whose roots were loose in the crumbling soil. For four or five seconds, no more, the white figures ran with slow, light steps on the stony edge of the road and then ran back from the road into the field of scrub and stone.

Their steps might have been normal. Perhaps they had only been frightened by the car. Perhaps it was their colour, robbing them of faces and even of nudity, that had made them seem light-footed and insubstantial. Perhaps it was the noise of the car, killing the cries they might have made and the sounds of their feet.

So brief an apparition, so abrupt and without disturbance: still listening for the helicopter above the beat of the engine, Bobby didn't look to see where in that bright rubbled landscape the chalked boys or men had gone. Linda didn't look. Neither she nor Bobby talked. And it was a little time before Bobby realized that the helicopter, for which he was listening, was no longer to be heard.

And now they were altogether out of the mountains, which began to show in the rear-view mirror as a blue-green range rising out of the bright plain. Farms appeared again, and fenced fields; little shack settlements at crossroads: houses and huts in dusty yards, two or three wooden shops: flaking distemper on old timber, faded advertisements on doors, twisted frames, dark interiors. They slowed down for a petrol tanker driven by an Indian. It was the first motor vehicle they had seen since leaving the hotel. But there were others now: old lorries, old cars driven by Africans. The road was tarred again. They were entering a market town.

Small ochre-and-red official buildings were scattered about the winding road. But the gaps between the buildings had not been filled; much of the town was waste-ground, as eroded and full of glare as a riverbed. The buildings were in a type of Italianate style, with a touch of the South American. Walls went right down to the ground and were mud-splashed; roughly plastered concrete looked like adobe. Crooked telegraph poles, sagging wires, the broken edges of the asphalt road, scuffed grass sidewalks, dust, scattered rubbish, African bicycles, broken-down lorries and motor cars outside the bus-station shed: the town had failed to grow, but it still worked.

Africans sat and squatted in a dusty park where eucalyptus had grown tall. There was a market with a little clock-tower. One stall was entirely hung with clothes for Africans, each garment on a hanger, the hangers staggered down and across, so that the stall appeared to be hung with a fluttering rag carpet. Below the clock on the tower there was, in raised concrete letters, red on ochre: MARKET 1951.

Then the town was past and the road was empty again. The road was so empty and the air so clear, the land so flat and stripped, that miles before they reached it they could see the embankment of the main highway to the Collectorate. And that too was empty. Black, wide and straight: the car stopped rattling. The tyres hissed again: the sound of smooth, swift motion. Air rushed through the half-open windows.

'Did you feel that?' Bobby was excited. 'You can get some dangerous crosswinds here. They blow you off the road if you aren't careful.'

The sun struck through the very top of the windscreen. Every deep scratch made the day before at the filling station was clear. On the gleaming bonnet minute scratches made circular patterns.

Linda said, 'I knew it.'

Beyond the white gleam of the bonnet, through the distortions of heatwaves, in the distance, black asphalt dissolving into light: a confusion of vehicles on one side of the road, an accident.

Linda said, 'I thought it was too good to be true. It always happens when the road is as empty as this.'

Approaching slowly, they saw a grey-and-magenta Volkswagen minibus parked level on the road; a blue Peugeot saloon parked on the verge; and, tilted to one side, half in the ditch, a shattered dark-green Peugeot estate-car, by its number-plate one of those used by Africans as long-distance taxis. There were other vehicles beyond this, but this was the only wreck: so new, in destruction so fragile and murderous.

As Bobby slowed down, an African in dark trousers and a white shirt came out from behind the minibus. Bobby stopped.

'Can we do anything to help?'

The African, squinting at the windscreen dazzle, looked uncertainly at Bobby and Linda and didn't reply.

Bobby edged forward past the fearful wreck. He saw a white Volkswagen; he stopped again. Like a hundred white Volkswagens; like the Volkswagen of yesterday; but the man who came around from behind it was not white and short, but black, tall, solidly made. Not the blackness or the stature of Africa: there was about his hard features and warm complexion something that suggested other bloods, another continent, another language.

Linda, looking at the wreck for blood, a body, shoes, a blanket, responded at once to the authority of this man. She leaned out into the sun and called to him, 'What's happened?'

He smiled at Linda and came close to the car.

'A fatal accident,' he said. 'Drive carefully.'

He was not of the country. He spoke with the unmistakable accent of the American Negro.

The smile and the accent, and the unexpected compassion of the advice, gave his words authority. Bobby felt the little thrill of human fellowship. It was something more than the sentimentality that overcame him whenever, innocent himself, and white, he met African officials or policemen doing a difficult duty. He was anxious to show that he obeyed, was responsive. He drove off carefully over the wavering black skid-marks that started and ended so abruptly on the black road. The sun was coming through the top of the scratched windscreen: he was aware of dazzle as a danger: he pulled down the visor.

The mirror showed activity around the estate-car and the minibus. There were more men than Bobby had noticed as he had passed. Then the road began to curve, and that view was lost.

Four or five army lorries, their axles high above the level road, were parked ahead. On the grass verge beside the lorries, in the shallow ditch, and in the shade of the stunted trees that grew in the field beyond, there were soldiers with rifles. Bobby drove slowly, to show that he had nothing to hide.

All the soldiers turned to look at the car. Below dark-green forage caps their black faces looked greased. The soldiers on the verge appeared to be frowning. Their eyes were narrow above their fat cheeks; foreheads that were so smooth during the entrancement of yesterday's run along the lake boulevard were now creased and puckered up between almost hairless eyebrows. Now they had guns in their hands, and no one else had. The soldiers beyond the ditch, in the shade of the trees, were smiling at the car.

Bobby lifted one hand from the steering-wheel in a half-wave. No one waved back. All the soldiers continued to look at the car, those who smiled, those who frowned.

Linda said, 'That wasn't an accident.'

Bobby was accelerating.

'Bobby, they've killed the king. That was the king.'

The road was straight and black. The tyres hissed on the wet tar.

'That was the king. They've killed him.'

'I don't know,' Bobby said.

'Those soldiers knew what they were grinning about. Did you see them grinning? Savages. Fat black savages. I can't bear it when they grin like that.'

'The king was black too.'

'Bobby, don't ask me to talk about that now.'

'I don't know what we're talking about. It probably was what that man said. An accident.'

'That would be nice to believe. You know, I thought it was a joke. They said he would try to get away in a taxi in some sort of disguise.'

'He must have picked it up around here somewhere. Between roadblocks.'

'That's what everybody in the capital was saying he would do. I thought it was a joke. And that's just what he goes and does.'

'Of course it was all bluff, all this talk about secession and an independent kingdom and so on. That was always Simon Lubero's private view, by the way. The king was just a London playboy. He impressed a lot of people over there. But I'm sorry to say he was a very foolish man.'

'That's what everybody says. And I suppose that's why I didn't believe it. I thought it was too foolish to be true. All that Oxford accent and London talk. I thought it was an act.'

'Simon was always level-headed about the whole thing. I happen to know that Simon very much wanted it to remain a purely police operation.'

'And yet you would think that these people would have their secret ways, that they would always be able to hide in the bush and get away. Being African and a king. I thought the helicopter and those white men in it were so ridiculous.'

'Yes,' Bobby said, 'the wogs got him.' His bitterness surprised him, the discovery of anger, aimed at no one. He became calmer. 'The wogs got him,' he said again. 'I hope the word gets back to London and I hope his smart friends find that funny too.'

He was still driving fast, but he was no longer racing.

He said, 'I should have telephoned Ogguna Wanga-Butere. He would have straightened out this curfew business. Not that I think there's going to be any trouble. We're making excellent time as it is.'

'You know what they say about Africa,' Linda said. 'You drive these long distances and when you get to where you're going there's nothing to do. But I must say I'm beginning to feel it would be nice to see the old compound again.'

The land opened out. The horizon dipped. Far away they could see the pale-blue hills, low, almost merging into the sky, and in the middle distance the isolated, curiously-shaped tors and cones, darker, greener, but still blurred in the haze, that marked this part of the Collectorate, the king's territory.

'Leopard Tor,' Linda said.

'It's one of my favourite views.'

'Like a John Ford western.'

'How very film-society. To me it's just Africa. There's going to be an awful lot of foolish talk in the compound in the next few weeks, and a lot of comment in the foreign press. I suppose I wouldn't mind it so much if I felt that those people really cared.'

'I don't know whether I care. That's the terrible thing. I don't know what I think. All I know is that I want to get back to the compound.'

Later, the view not changing in spite of their speed, distances appearing to remain what they were, Linda said, 'Why do you suppose they call it Leopard Tor?'

Bobby noted that her voice had altered and was growing mystical. He didn't reply.

She said, 'I saw a dead leopard once.'

Bobby concentrated on the road.

'In West Africa. A long red tongue hanging down from between the teeth. I wanted to touch it when they brought it in, to see if it was still warm. But you mustn't, because it's full of fleas. Then they began to skin it. Just below the skin it was like a ballet dancer in tights. You wouldn't believe the muscles. All that had to be cut up and thrown away, burnt on the fire. In the morning when I got up I thought, "I'll go and look at the leopard." I'd forgotten.'

She spoke slowly. She had begun to listen to her own words.

Bobby said, 'I don't believe they're going to skin the king.'

'I can't bear it the way those soldiers grin. Did you see them grinning? You weren't here for the mutiny. Eighty marines flew in. Just eighty, and those same grinning soldiers threw away their guns and tore off those uniforms and ran off naked into the bush. They could run in those days. They weren't so fat. It was funny at the airport. Everybody from the compound was there. But the marines weren't waving back. Those young boys were just jumping out of the planes, guns at the ready, and running through the applauding crowd.'

'I heard about that,' Bobby said. 'I don't think the Africans have forgotten either. They find it rather less funny. It's their big fear, you know, since the Belgians and the Congo. White men coming down from the sky.'

'That's what Sammy Kisenyi was telling me.'

'That's what many of them thought the king wanted.'

'I feel like the colonel. I feel I should have gone out and done something to help the king. But then I know that wouldn't have made much sense either.'

'That's just it. It's not your business or mine. They have to sort these things out themselves. And he nearly made it, you know. If he hadn't been spotted, in another ninety minutes or so he would have been up there, scuttling across the lake to the other side.'

'Oh my God. You mean they're still waiting for him at the lake? They must have been waiting all last night. It's going to be awful in the Collectorate when the news breaks.'

'I imagine they'll keep it quiet for a day or two.'

'I feel I never want to stir out of the compound again.'

'That would be quite a departure, for you.'

'Of course,' Linda said, responding to the provocation, 'the soldiers may be rampaging around there at this minute.'

The wide view was going. The land was becoming more broken; there were more trees; the road curved more often. They passed allotments, shops, huts: a village. But no one was to be seen.

'I hated this place from the first day I came here,' Linda said. 'I felt I had no right to be among these people. It was too easy. They made it too easy. It wasn't at all what I wanted.'

Bobby said, 'You know why you came.'

'They sent Jimmy Ruhengiri to meet us at the airport. For forty miles I had to make conversation with Jimmy. The conversation you make with the educated ones. Like playing chess with yourself: you make all the moves. And all I kept on seeing were those horrible little huts. I was screaming inside. I knew that nothing good was going to happen to me here. And that first day they put us up in a filthy room in the barracks they call a guest-house. Martin didn't have enough points. We didn't know. Give Martin a points-system to live by, and you can be sure Martin will never have enough points for anything.'

'You didn't do too badly,' Bobby said.

'A girl in the next room was crying, and it was still only afternoon. That really frightened me. I don't think I ever wanted anything so much as I wanted to leave that day, to go back to the airport and take the next plane back to London.'

'Why didn't you?'

'You go out driving with Sammy Kisenyi, making educated conversation, and you see a naked savage with a penis one foot long. You pretend you've seen nothing. You see two naked boys painted white running about the public highway, and you don't talk about it. Sammy Kisenyi reads a paper on broadcasting at the conference. He's lifted whole paragraphs from T. S. Eliot, of all people. You say nothing about it, you can't say anything about it. Outside you encourage and encourage. In the compound you talk and talk. Everybody just lies and lies and lies.'

'You know why you came. You can't complain.'

'It's their country. But it's your life. In the end you don't know what you feel about anything. All you know is that you want to be safe in the compound.'

'You came for the freedom, though. You adjust very easily, remember?'

'No doubt we look at these things differently, Bobby.'

'It doesn't matter now what you think, though.'

'Every night in the compound you hear them raising the hue and cry, and you know they're beating someone to death outside. Every week there's this list of people who've been killed, and some of them don't even have names. You should either stay away, or you should go among them with the whip in your hand. Anything in between is ridiculous.'

'Is that Martin? Or the colonel? I can't keep up with you, Linda. All those lovely weekends in the capital, with all those lovely open fires. Somehow I was expecting more. I was astonished at your taste, Linda. "I adjust very easily." Very nicely spoken, but it's nobody's fault if the people we find are just like ourselves. You've all been reading the same books. Of course, we read a lot, don't we? We mustn't let our minds grow rusty, among the savages.'

'It isn't for you to talk like this, Bobby.'

'I'm disqualified, am I? You should have told me. But I

thought you wanted a houseboy to spread the news. I thought you wanted someone to excite by your screams in bed.'

'That is one of Doris Marshall's absurd stories.'

'"Let's get Bobby to witness. He is one of Denis Marshall's."' He was moving his head up and down. '"Let's get Bobby. You can do what you like with Bobby." "That's a nice shirt you're wearing, Bobby." Very funny. But you chose the wrong man.'

'This is nonsense.'

'Is it?' He took his right hand off the steering-wheel and tapped his head. 'I notice everything. It's all there.'

'I always thought you were a romantic, Bobby.'

'You chose the wrong man.'

'I wish it was the way you tell it. You can't have looked very carefully at the people in the compound.'

'That's just it. It's nobody's fault if the people you find are just like yourself.'

'Let's stop this, Bobby. I take back everything.'

'You talk about savages and whips.'

'I take that back.'

'There are so many like you, Linda. We mustn't let our minds grow rusty. We are among savages and we need our cultural activities. We are among these very dirty savages and we must remind ourselves that we have this loveliness. Do we use our vaginal deodorant daily?'

'This is ridiculous.'

'*Do we? Do we?* What brand do we use? Hot Girl, Cool Girl, Fresh Girl? Girl-Fresh? You're nothing. You're nothing but a rotting cunt. There are millions like you, millions, and there will be millions more. "I'm very adjustable." "I hope they've done nothing to the poor wives." I don't know who you think you are. I don't know why you think it matters what you think about anything.'

She leaned back in her seat and looked out of her window. A village again: dusty shacks, tropical backyard vegetation, a dirt side road: a vista of sun, dust and trees there; and then bush beside the highway again.

'There are millions like you. And millions like Martin. You are *nothing*.'

'Please stop the car. I will get out here. I don't want to say anything more. Please stop the car.'

He braked with a squeal on the hot road. The wind stopped rushing through the windows. The beat of the engine was like silence. Trees were throwing squat shadows across the ditches. The sky was hot and high.

Linda said, 'You were right. It wasn't a good idea.'

'You're a fool. You'll get into trouble.'

'I'm very foolish.'

'This is your idea, remember.'

'I'll make other arrangements. I'll probably get a taxi or something.'

As she turned to open the door he saw that the back of her shirt was wet. He was aware then that his own shirt was wet, and felt cold. For a second, stepping out on the road, Linda appeared to be without a sense of direction. Her dark glasses masked her expression. She steadied herself. Bobby watched her start back towards the village they had just passed.

He called, 'Your suitcase?'

She didn't turn. 'You can take that.'

He opened his door and stood up on the road. The sense of the moving road remained with him. He felt dizzy in the still hot air; he had again that sensation of the overcharged, exploding head.

'Linda!'

She continued to walk away with her brisk little steps, looking down, so alien on the high embankment of the empty road, so accidental-looking, the colours of her trousers and shirt suddenly so bright and noticeable that vivid colour seemed to come as well to the road and fields and sky, and the scene had something of the unreal quality of a colour photograph.

He got back in the car, slammed the door shut and drove off, rubbing his dry palms on the steering-wheel, studying the black road, feeling the heat thrown back from the bonnet, where the sun was reflected in a little ring of scratched glitter.

*

Minutes later, aware all the time of the declining sun, the black shadows of trees, the empty fields, the empty car, the roar of the engine and the wind, he began to have the sense of nightmare. The colonel and the hotel, the soldier beside the wide riverbed, the white boys breaking out into the road like heraldic animals and running in slow, silent motion, Linda on the road: the pictures were clear, they had a sequence, but they were like things imagined.

He needed to be calmer. Acknowledging the need, he became calmer. The sense of nightmare was reduced to a memory of his own violence and a foreboding of danger. He was alone; he was inviting reprisal. But still he raced. There was danger at the end of the road, danger in his solitude. But still he allowed time to pass.

The car jumped, came down hard again on the road, and the steering-wheel momentarily kicked itself free of his hands. The road here had subsided. The thin asphalt crust, soft and melting in the afternoon sun, rose and fell. It was a stretch of road Bobby knew. He took his foot off the accelerator. Another bump, another slither, but he was in control. He stopped, and again was aware of the silence, the light, the heat.

He turned to go back. The road was as empty as before. On the wet tar he saw the tracks he had just made. In his panic, the road and the fields had been like things he was imagining. It astonished him, going back, to find he had seen it so clearly and remembered so much. His car had made perfect tracks, quite ordinary.

There was no sign of Linda on the highway. The little village that had been built all on one side of the highway, about the dirt road, looked shut up and evacuated. No one appeared when Bobby sounded his horn. The two or three shops, crooked wooden structures, were the colour of their bare, dusty yards. On tin advertisements nailed to the closed doors, the sheets of tin robbed by the sunlight of all colours except black and pale yellow, a laughing African woman in a turban-type headdress held up a jar of eczema ointment and a laughing African man smoked a cigarette.

Bobby turned into the dirt road. At once there was dust. At once all that the rear-view mirror showed was dust, dense and billowing, like the yellow smoke from a fierce fire. Bobby closed the windows; but as he drove along, obliterating what he had seen, bush, tall trees, an empty wooden hut, the dust in the car became thicker. He saw a large corrugated-iron shed standing in a junk-yard, old grease black and thick on dust; and next to this, behind two or three starved shrubs in hard earth, a white concrete bungalow on low pillars, squarely exposed to the afternoon sun.

Bobby stopped and rolled down his window. Dust billowed slowly around the car. When Bobby sounded his horn, a lanky Indian youth opened the front door of the bungalow. He looked at the car, and beckoned. Bobby hesitated. The boy stood where he was, between verandah and inner room, a puzzled intermediary between Bobby and someone inside.

Bobby went into the bungalow. The verandah, an afternoon sun-trap, heat reflected from white walls and rising from the floorboards, was empty. In the suffocating little drawing-room, among paper flowers and paperbacks, chairs with chromium-plated metal frames and Hindu deities in copper-coloured plastic, Linda appeared to be having tea. With bared teeth she was biting the very tip of a pickled chili.

Bobby ignored the middle-aged Indian, Linda's host, and said, 'We don't have too much time now.'

Linda said, 'I'm having a little tea.'

'Well, I suppose there's no rush. I suppose I'll have a little tea too.'

'Yes, yes,' the middle-aged Indian said, and went out of the room.

Neither Bobby nor Linda nor the tall boy spoke. It was very hot. Linda was red; Bobby began to sweat. A young woman in a green sari brought a plate of pickles and an extra cup, and went out again.

'Nice place you have here,' Bobby said, when the middle-aged man returned.

'Mrs McCartland,' the man said, sitting down and rocking his legs from side to side. 'She sold up in a hurry when she went South. House, furniture, books, business, everything.'

Bobby said, 'Nice books.'

'You want a few?' His legs still, the man leaned towards the bookcase and pulled out a handful of paperbacks with his left hand. 'Take.'

Bobby shook his head. 'Are you going South too?'

The man giggled and pushed the books back in place. 'I am thinking of cloth business in the United States. Or Cairo. I am starting a juices-parlour in Cairo.'

'What's that?'

'These Egyptians, you see, are drinking so much of the fresh fruit juices. As soon as I can get my money out, I will go. My brother is already there. Where are you going?'

'I live here,' Bobby said. 'I'm a government officer.'

Slowly, the man's legs stopped rocking. He giggled.

Linda got up. 'I think we should be starting.'

Bobby smiled and sipped his tea.

'You knew Mr McCartland?' the man asked, after a time.

'I didn't know him.' Bobby stood up.

'He died when he was very young,' the man said, following Bobby and Linda out into the yard and the road, where the dust was still settling. 'He was a great racer. He used to drive early in the mornings from here to the capital at a hundred miles an hour.'

Bobby, walking slowly, looking up at the sky, not acknowledging the man's farewells, said, 'That's what we'll have to do now to get to the Collectorate before the curfew.'

They got into the car. The Indian went up to his verandah and watched them reverse in the garage yard. The dust began to billow again. When they drove away dust blotted out the road.

Linda said, 'Do you believe that man drove to the capital at a hundred miles an hour?'

'Do you?'

'I wonder why he said that.'

At the junction the shops were as closed and blank as before. The bleached Africans on the tin advertisements grinned; shadows had lengthened below the eaves.

They turned into the highway and rolled down their windows. The sun slanted through the scratched dusty windscreen. Everything in the car was coated with dust; on the dashboard every little grain of dust cast a minute shadow. On the soft tar, on the righthand side of the road, Bobby saw one of the tracks he had made when he had driven back to the village. All his other tracks had been obliterated, by treads of a chunkier pattern. More than one heavy vehicle had passed, keeping more or less to the left, heading towards the Collectorate.

Bobby drove cautiously. He came again to the stretch of subsidence where the road, soft tar on an uneven surface, appeared to billow and melt. Here was where he had stopped:

something still remained of the curving tracks where he had turned.

'Are we very late?' Linda said.

'We've only lost about half an hour. But I imagine you'll smile sweetly at them and they'll give us a cup of tea.'

They both smiled, as though they had both won.

At first with private smiles, and then with fixed faces, they drove through the hot afternoon air, shadows beginning to fall on the road, slanting towards them from the right; and neither of them exclaimed when, abruptly, they saw Leopard Tor again, nearer now and larger, half in sun and half in shadow, its vertical wall less sheer, its sloping side, tufted with forest, more jagged.

Linda said, 'Do you believe he's really going to Cairo?'

'He's lying,' Bobby said. 'Everybody lies.'

She smiled.

Then she saw what Bobby was gazing at, at the end of the road: the column of army lorries whose tyre-tracks they had been following.

9

He hung back. He speeded up. He hung back again. Neither
he nor Linda spoke. Leopard Tor, rising out of bush, was
always to the right, its forested slope in shadow. The vegetation beside the highway had subtly altered. It was still scrub; no
crops grew on it; but it was acquiring a rainy tropical lushness.
They came nearer and nearer the lorries, a column of five, their
slanting shadows falling just over the asphalt and jigging along
the irregularities of the verge. Sometimes, through a break in
the vegetation, Bobby and Linda could see the purely tropical
land beyond the Tor, the territory of the king's people, a vast
sunlit woodland, seemingly empty, with only scattered patches
of a browner haze to show where, in that bush, the villages
were.

The green-capped soldiers sitting with rifles at the back
of the last lorry scowled at the car. The faces of the soldiers
behind them were in shadow. Then Bobby saw the driver.
His face and his cap, shakily reflected in profile in the wing-
mirror of the cab, made a featureless black outline against a

background of dazzle. Sometimes, when the lorry bumped, or when he turned to look at the mirror and Bobby, the face caught a yellow shine from the sun.

So for a time Bobby and Linda drove on, keeping at a fixed distance from the last lorry. Behind the tailboard, with its heraldic regimental emblem, the soldiers continued to scowl. Intermittently Bobby felt the gaze of the driver; every now and then that face in the mirror shone.

Linda said, 'If we go on at this rate we'll certainly be late.'

'It's not easy to overtake on this road,' Bobby said. 'It winds so much.'

They drove on. The soldiers continued to stare.

Linda said, 'We're probably making them anxious.'

Bobby didn't smile.

They came to a stretch of road that was straight and undeniably clear.

Bobby sounded his horn and pulled out to overtake. The soldiers became alert. Bobby, accelerating, looked up at them, looked away, too quickly, and was dazzled by the sun. He began to overtake, sounding his horn. The lorry moved to the right. Spots streamed before Bobby's eyes; he raced; he was already almost off the road. The lorry continued to move to the right. Bobby was driving beside it. He felt his right wheels mount the verge. The ditch came close. He braked and the car bucked and bumped. The lorry pulled away. The soldiers' faces creased into friendly smiles. The cab-mirror reflected the driver's laugh: suddenly he had a face. Then that reflection was lost. The car was askew on the verge. The lorry moved further away, fell back into line. The soldiers' faces became indistinct. A khaki-clad arm came out from the driver's cab and flapped about awkwardly, hand swinging from the wrist: it was a signal to overtake.

Linda said, 'When you meet the army, play dead.'

The back of Bobby's shirt was wet. His face began to burn. He felt the heat of the engine, the bonnet, the windscreen. The air was warm; the floor of the car was warm. Hot sweat broke out afresh all over his body. His eyes pricked; his trousers stuck to his shins.

He started the car and took it off the verge. Once more he followed the tracks of the lorries, chunky zipper-patterns on the soft asphalt. He drove slowly, never more than thirty-five miles an hour; and still from time to time they saw the lorries. The Tor grew larger; haze softened its shadowed forested slope. The afternoon light grew smoky.

And now the highway opened up, and for miles ahead was as straight as a Roman road, swinging from hill to hill. The army lorries, small in the distance, climbed, disappeared, and then were seen to climb again. They were entering the territory of the king's people; and the highway here followed the ancient forest road. For centuries, using only the products of the forest, earth, reeds, the king's people had built their roads as straight as this, over hills, across swamps. From far away Bobby could see the small white-washed stone building, a police post, that stood at the boundary of the king's territory. But the flag that flew there today wasn't the king's flag. It was the flag of the president's country.

Near the stone building the lorries turned off the road, and the road was empty again. But Bobby didn't drive any faster.

There was no longer any point; it was past four, the hour of the curfew. Soon they could see the low, sprawling modern building, glass and coloured concrete, as bright as beads, that the Americans had built in the bush as a gift to the new country. It had been intended as a school, and symbolically it straddled the king's territory and the president's. It had been visited but never used; there had been neither pupils nor teachers; it had remained empty. It had a use today. The cleared space in front, partly bushed-over again, was full of lorries. And in the shade of the lorries there were groups of fat soldiers.

No barrier stood in the road here; no one waved them down. But Bobby stopped: the school, the lorries and the soldiers to his left, the stone building, over which the president's flag flew, across the road to his right. The soldiers didn't look at the car. No one came out of the stone building. Beyond the Tor was bright woodland, extending to the horizon through a deepening smoke haze.

'Do we wait for them here?' Linda said.

Bobby didn't reply.

'Perhaps there's no curfew,' Linda said.

A soldier was looking at them. He was shorter than the soldiers he stood with, near the open tailboard of a lorry. He was drinking from a tin cup.

'Perhaps the colonel got it wrong,' Linda said.

'*Did* he?' Bobby said.

The soldier moved away from the group by the tailboard, shook out his tin cup, and walked slowly towards the car. His head was shaved and bare. His stiff khaki trousers were creased below his paunch and down the round thighs that rubbed against one another. He sucked at the inside of his fat cheeks and bunched his lips and spat, carefully, leaning to one side to let the spittle drain out from his lips. He smiled at the car.

Then they saw the prisoners. They were sitting on the ground; some were prostrate; most were naked. It was their nakedness that had camouflaged them in the sun-and-shade about the shrubs, small trees and lorries. Bright eyes were alive in black flesh; but there was little movement among the prisoners. They were the slender, small-boned, very black people of the king's tribe, a clothed people, builders of roads. But such dignity as they had possessed in freedom had already gone; they were only forest people now, in the hands of their enemies. Some were roped up in the traditional forest way, neck to neck, in groups of three or four, as though for delivery to the slave-merchant. All showed the liver-coloured marks of blood and beatings. One or two looked dead.

The soldier smiled, wet hand holding the wet tin cup, and came near the car.

Bobby, preparing a smile, leaned across Linda and, with his left hand freeing the wet native shirt from his left armpit, asked, 'Who your officer? Who your boss-man?'

Linda looked away from the soldier to the whitewashed stone building and the flag, the Tor and the smoking woodland.

The soldier pressed his belly against the car door and the smell of his warm khaki mingled with the smell of the sweat from Bobby's open left armpit and his yellow back. The soldier looked at Bobby and Linda and looked into the car, and spoke softly in a complicated forest language.

'Who your boss-man?' Bobby asked again.

'Let's drive on, Bobby,' Linda said. 'They're not interested in us. Let's drive on.'

Bobby pointed to the stone building. 'Boss-man there?'

The soldier spoke again, this time to Linda, in his language.

She said irritably, 'I don't understand,' and looked straight ahead.

The soldier behaved as though he had been slapped. He gave a sheepish smile and took a step back from the car. He shook out his tin cup; he stopped smiling. He said softly, *'Don' un'erstan'. Don' un'erstan'.'* He looked down at the body of the car, the doors, the wheels, as though searching for something. Then he turned and began to walk back to his group.

Bobby opened his door and got out. It was cool; the sweated shirt was chill on his back; but the tar was soft below his feet. He could see the prisoners more clearly now. He could see the smoke from the woodland beyond the Tor. Not haze, not afternoon cooking-fires: in that bush, villages were on fire. The rebuffed soldier was talking to his comrades. Bobby tried not to see. His instinct was to get back in the car and drive without stopping to the compound. But he controlled himself. Quickly, right hand swinging, he crossed the bright road into the dusty yard and the shadow cast by the stone building, and went through the open door.

As soon as he entered he knew he had made a mistake. But it was too late to withdraw. In the cool dark room, with its desks and chairs pushed to the walls, with the new photograph of the president on the green noticeboard, among old notices about rates and taxes and wanted criminals and other printed and duplicated lists, there was no officer, no policeman. Three soldiers with shaved heads were sitting below the window on the concrete floor, their caps on their knees. They all stood up as Bobby entered.

'I'm a government officer,' Bobby said.

'Sir!' one of the soldiers said, and they all stood to attention.

'Who your officer? Who your boss-man?'

They didn't reply and Bobby didn't know how, after his good start, to continue.

They saw his hesitation and they ceased to be nervous. They relaxed. Their faces became full of inquiry.

The soldier in the middle said, 'No boss-man.'

Bobby felt he had used the wrong word. He looked from the soldier in the middle to the soldier on the right, the fattest of the three, the one who had called him sir. 'You give pass here?'

The fat soldier's cheeks rode up to his small liquid eyes. He waved his right hand slowly in front of his face, showing Bobby the palm.

'No pass,' the soldier in the middle said.

Bobby looked at him. 'Mr Wanga-Butere *my* boss-man.' Smiling, he held his hands in front of him to indicate an enormous paunch, and he pretended to stagger under the weight. 'Mr Busoga-Kesoro my *big* boss-man.'

They didn't smile.

'Busoga-Kesoro,' the fat soldier said, studying Bobby's face, and working his cheeks and lips as though gathering spittle. 'Busoga-Kesoro.'

'You no have curfew?' Bobby said.

'Car-few,' the fat soldier said.

The soldier in the middle said, 'Car-few.'

'What time you have car-few? Four o'clock, five o'clock, six o'clock?'

'Five o'clock,' the fat soldier said. 'Six o'clock.'

Bobby held out his wrist and pointed to his watch. 'Four? Five? Six?'

'You give me?' the fat soldier said, and held Bobby's wrist. Black skin on pink: they all looked.

The fat soldier moved his thumb over the dial of the watch. His eyes were friendly, womanish. His cheeks and lips began to work again.

The soldier in the middle unbuttoned the pocket of his tunic and took out a crushed, half-empty packet of cigarettes. It was the brand which, in the advertisements, laughing Africans smoked.

Outside, lorries were revving up. There was chatter and shouting. Boots grated on asphalt; cab-doors slammed. Lorries whined away in low gear.

'I no give you,' Bobby said. 'I no have no more.'

He had made a joke. They all laughed.

'No have no more,' the fat soldier said, and let Bobby's wrist drop.

'I go,' Bobby said.

He walked towards the door. He had a view of the sunlit road, the dusty yard with its diagonal line of shadow, the insect-spattered front of his car.

'Boy!'

He stopped; it was his error. He turned, to face the dark room.

It was the soldier in the middle who had spoken. He was

holding out an unlit cigarette, very white, between his middle and index fingers.

'I give you cigarette, boy.'

'I no smoke,' Bobby said.

'I give you. Come, I give you.'

And Bobby walked from the door and the brightness towards the soldiers, preferring that what was going to happen should happen here, in the dark room, rather than in the open, before the others.

The soldier's hand was outstretched still, open, palm down, the cigarette perpendicular between the middle and index fingers. Then the fingers widened, the cigarette fell, and in that same movement of finger-widening the palm came up at Bobby's face, only clawing, it seemed, but then landing hard on his chin. The other hand tore at the yellow native shirt.

'I report you,' Bobby said, falling back. 'I report you.'

The other soldiers were behind him, to support him as he fell, to seize and twist his arms with practised hands; and it seemed then that the soldier in front of him was maddened not by his words but by the sound and sight of the torn shirt. He tore again and again at the shirt and the vest below the shirt, and with the right hand that had held the cigarette he clawed with clumsy rage at Bobby's face as though wishing to seize it by the nose, chin and cheeks alone.

'I report you,' Bobby said.

His arms were twisted harder and he was thrown forward, and when he was on the concrete floor, feeling the boots thump him on the back, the neck, the jaw, he saw, with surprise, that the legs of two soldiers were quite still. It was the fat soldier, grunting as he squatted, tight in his khaki, who was beside him, seizing him by the hair, banging his head on the floor, rubbing his face hard on the floor, now this side, now the other. Bobby knew he was losing skin; but still he noticed that the other soldiers remained where they were.

He had thought at first that the soldier with the cigarette wished only to humiliate, denude, disfigure; and he had half understood, half felt sympathy. But they had gone too far; and now he felt that the fat soldier, who had asked for the watch, intended to kill. He thought: I must protect myself, I must play dead.

Sprawling on his front, he made himself heavy, his left arm jammed against the side of his head. The boots probed his ribs, his belly, probed and kicked. Bobby tried not to move; he didn't think he moved; the fine grit on the smooth plaster of the floor stuck to his wet skin. He didn't open his eyes, fearing to find that he might not be able to see. Then he felt the boot hard on his right wrist, and he could have cried then, at the clear pure pain, the knowledge of the fracture, so deliberate, the knowledge that what had been whole all his life had been broken. He shut out everything to concentrate on that wrist. He felt it grow numb; he felt the swelling come. And then he was on the road again, in a bright landscape, nervous at his own speed, his tyre-tracks and the wet, billowing road.

He awakened. He thought he would open his eyes. His whole face burned. He could see. He could see that in the dark room there were no more khaki legs. He waited to make sure. He felt it was important to act at once, while he was lucid, while the strength that had come back to him remained. He sat up, leaning on his wrist. He had forgotten that injury; he remembered now. He stood up, and he was steady. He didn't look at himself. Walking, he remembered to look on the floor. But he didn't see the cigarette the soldier had dropped.

The light was yellower. Shadows had spread and were less harsh. There was more dust and smoke. The sun caught the windscreen of a lorry, a window of the school. Soldiers squatted or sat around small twig fires, eating out of tin plates, drinking out of tin cups, unhurried, deliberate, their eyes and voices bright with the pleasure of food: forest people, kings of the forest, at the end of another lucky day. Some way behind them, in the sun, the bound black prisoners lay on the ground and didn't move.

A soldier saw Bobby and stared. The soldier's eyes glittered. Without turning his head he spoke to the man beside him, and the whole group looked. Bobby held his hands at his side and stood in the doorway, allowing himself to be examined. He began to walk to the car, which remained where he had left it, quite exposed on the open road, the wheels slightly sunk in the asphalt. The soldiers went back to their food.

Linda, still in her seat, leaned to hold the door open. No one came to the car. The engine answered. Bobby rested his right hand on the steering-wheel. No one stopped him from leaving. The afternoon light made every scratch on the windscreen gold. The almost perpendicular side of Leopard Tor was also gold; the shadowed side was blurred, the forest on its lower slopes now like part of the surrounding bush.

Four or five hundred yards away, over the brow of the hill, they came to the roadblock. The soldier with the rifle, his face just black below his cap, waved them down with the awkward flapping African gesture. But even before they stopped, the man in the flowered shirt and dark trousers and his hair in the English style, on the other side of the road, signalled to them to go on.

Bobby drove in and out of the white barriers and then slowly past the vehicles halted on the other side of the road, vehicles going out of the Collectorate: the Peugeot taxi-buses, the broken-down vans and African cars. The passengers were on the verge. Some were holding duplicated foolscap sheets, their passes; but others were already sitting down or lying on the grass, half naked, their clothes torn; the fully clothed soldiers moved among them. Some of the African women were in Edwardian costumes. So the first missionaries had appeared among the king's people; and so, ever since, but in African-style cottons, the women of the king's people had dressed on formal occasions or whenever they made a long journey.

The road continued straight, from hilltop to hilltop, a strip of asphalt in a wide swathe through the bush.

Linda said, 'Let's stop for a little, Bobby.'

He pulled up on the road, just like that.

She tried to dust his hair, to straighten the rags of the yellow shirt. There was little else she could do. He didn't allow her to touch his face.

She said, 'Your watch is broken.'

Bobby closed his heavy eyes and, in that darkness, thought, with sudden passing sorrow for her, for whom so much had also gone wrong: but these are the hands of a nurse.

He opened his eyes and saw the road. They drove on. The

sky above was dark blue; the light was beginning to go. The tufted forest glowed where the king's villages were burning.

They were a people who lived, vulnerably now, in villages along their ancient straight roads: roads that had spread their power as forest conquerors, until the first explorers came. The villages were close together; the highway was normally full of pedestrians and cyclists. But the road now was empty; and the villages they passed were empty, dead, burnt-out. The villages that blazed were in the dirt tracks off the main road.

Linda said, 'I wonder if they've burned down the compound.'

But there was no other place to drive to.

The road dipped; they lost the view of the burning villages. The bush was tall and dark in this depression. They had entered forest, and the road, a straight black cutting, swung away between walls of forest, up and down, and then up to a high horizon. Bobby's wrist ached; he felt his eyes grow heavy. And then he was in a white storm. Like flakes of snow they came out of the forest, butterflies, white, on the asphalt, on the grass, on tree trunks, in the air, millions and millions of white butterflies, fluttering out of the forest. And the storm did not stop. They were crushed by the car wheels; they touched the bonnet and fluttered on the hot metal and died; they stuck to the windscreen.

Linda worked the washer; she turned on the wipers.

The road rose. The butterflies stopped as suddenly as they had begun. The forest ended. The sky above was the darkest blue. In the distance they saw the villages burning around the

small town, showing in the quick dusk as a few broken lines of lights.

Bobby said, 'I believe something's happened to my wrist.'

'I wish I could drive.'

He heard the panic in Linda's voice, and he didn't care. The road continued empty, the villages they passed gutted. Collapsed huts of mud and grass would have seemed part of the bush; corrugated iron made a ruin. Here and there women and children had returned to the ruins, the women plump in the manner of the women of the king's people, looking over-dressed in their Edwardian costumes. The car drove itself; and it didn't surprise Bobby, now only following the headlights of the car, that the women, shiny-faced with fatigue, should be where they were; or that in the little industrial estate just out-side the town there should still be electricity and illuminated signboards; or that where once, behind its high double walls, the king's palace glowed dully there should be darkness.

The walls had been breached; there was destruction inside: lorries, soldiers, campfires. To that ancient site, less than a hun-dred years before, the first explorers had brought news of the world beyond the forest. Now the site had its first true ruin, a palace built mostly in the 1920s, the first palace built there of materials less perishable than reeds and grass.

Between the palace and the colonial town was an open, indeterminate area: caravanserai, rubbish dump, pasture-land, market place, shanty town. Few lights burned there. Wholesale warehouses, traffic lights: road signs became complicated. Army lorries and jeeps stood at some intersections. Sometimes the headlights picked out the green cap and shining face of a

dazzled soldier. But no awkward hand waved Bobby down. In the main street, where half a dozen three- or four-storeyed concrete buildings rose above the old pioneer wooden structures of the original Indian-English settlement, some Indian furniture shops had been looted. But most of the shops were boarded up and whole.

After the main street the town was open again: a park, looking across to the scattered lights of the main residential area; a roundabout, with soldiers; then, straight ahead, going out of the town again, into the darkness again, towards the glowing sky, another nondescript African area, houses and huts and roadside standpipes, motor-repair yards with decrepit lorries, shops and stalls and backyard vegetable plots, stretching all the way to the compound. Usually this road was busy, and at this time of evening dangerous with drunks or Africans from the deep bush who hadn't yet learned to assess the speed of motor vehicles. Now it was clear. But the road was rough, potholed after the rains, and bumpy with asphalt that had melted and run together and grown hard. At every bump Bobby grew weaker.

Trees screened the compound from the road. At the end of the short drive two dim globes burned above the pillars of the iron gates. The gates were closed; the red-and-white wooden barrier was down. Bobby stopped. A torchlight flashed inches away from his face, and just outside the dazzle he saw lorries and soldiers.

The torchlight played about the windscreen, smeared with the yellow-white mess of mangled butterflies, and rested on the compound pass stuck on the inside.

'*Boswa et bévéni. M'sé, mem.*'

It was one of the compound watchmen, offering a laughing welcome in the patois which was his distinction and his pride. He was neither of the king's people nor the president's. He came from another country; in the Collectorate he was neutral, a spectator, and as safe as the compound he watched over.

The compound was safe. The soldiers were there to protect it. The wooden barrier flew up, and the watchman, in his old-fashioned red-and-blue uniform, ran to open the gate, as though anxious to display his zeal, and the authority of the people he served, to the watching soldiers. He pushed half the gate inwards and held it open; he saluted as the car passed in; and then he ran with the gate to close it again.

The big compound road-map was illuminated. The neatly labelled streets, artificially winding through the compound's landscaped grounds, were well lit. Fluorescent light fell on hedges and gardens. The open windows of bungalows and flats showed bark-cloths and straw-work on walls. African paintings, bookshelves. The little clubhouse was crowded.

Linda said, 'How's your wrist?'

Bobby didn't answer. Linda's voice was lighter, brisker; he could tell her panic had gone. The compound was her setting; she had news.

*

Intermittently during the night Bobby awoke from the drive and the confused dangers of the road to the comfort of bandages. As it grew lighter he began to wait for Luke, his houseboy. He was awakened by radios from the boys' quarters. Then he was awakened by the sound of Luke's brisk bare feet in the next

room. There was guilt in that briskness; and when Luke tiptoed into the bedroom, his shrunken khaki trousers catching in the crotch and high above his small ankles, Bobby could tell, from the delicacy of his steps and from Luke's crumpled white shirt, that Luke had been drinking and had slept in his clothes.

Luke drew the curtains and said in his heavy, drunken voice, 'Blue Dress out in garden this morning.' This was one of their private jokes, about a compound wife, an American and a newcomer, who for several weeks had appeared to wear the same blue dress.

Then Luke turned and saw Bobby. He stood where he was and pulled in his lips hard. Luke was of the king's people and came from one of the nearby villages; he knew the ways of the president's army. His red eyes stared; his nostrils widened and his long, thin face quivered. He sniffed; his pulled-in lips flapped open. With a snort, and with swift little stamps of his right foot, he began to laugh.

Afterwards, still briskly, but now without his delicacy, moving as though he was alone and unobserved, he gathered up Bobby's travelling clothes.

Bobby thought: I will have to leave. But the compound was safe; the soldiers guarded the gate. Bobby thought: I will have to sack Luke.

picador.com

blog
videos
interviews
extracts